GUSTAV GLOOM

AND THE CASTLE OF FEAR

by Adam-Troy Castro
illustrated by Kristen Margiotta

Grosset & Dunlap
An Imprint of Penguin Random House

GROSSET & DUNLAP
Penguin Young Readers Group
An Imprint of Penguin Random House LLC

Text copyright © 2016 by Adam-Troy Castro. Illustrations copyright © 2016 by Kristen Margiotta. All rights reserved. Published by Grosset & Dunlap, an imprint of Penguin Random House LLC, 345 Hudson Street, New York, New York 10014. GROSSET & DUNLAP is a trademark of Penguin Random House LLC. Manufactured in China.

Library of Congress Cataloging-in-Publication Data is available.

ISBN 9780448464596   10 9 8 7 6 5 4 3 2 1

To Jonathan Lowell,

and to Elisheva and Yael,

and to all children still

too young for these words:

Never Let Your Imagination Rest.

CHAPTER ONE
THE RETURN OF THE PEOPLE TAKER

Once upon a time, there was a very awful man by the name of Ernest J. Throckworthy.

There is no particular reason to remember that name, silly as it was, because he stopped using it very early on in life and after a while might not have been able to recall it himself. It's much more helpful to refer to him by the name he used for himself, whenever he was out and about doing terrible things: the People Taker.

It was under this title that he spent many years doing monstrous things in the world of light, and then later on many years serving an even more horrific master, Lord Obsidian.

It was also under this ominous job title that he twice fought the very brave young boy named Gustav Gloom, and Gustav's best friend, the not quite as strange but just as brave young girl named Fernie What.

1

Neither of these confrontations worked out at all well for the People Taker, which is why he now found himself imprisoned in one of the most aggravating of the Gloom mansion's many chambers.

The Room of Being Delayed Indefinitely resembled every waiting room anybody had ever had to spend an unwanted hour in, complete with uncomfortable chairs, magazines nobody would ever want to read, and a wall clock that ticked constantly but somehow never progressed past 3:24. Neither of the two doors, facing each other on opposite walls, ever opened. Maybe they couldn't open.

The People Taker spent what felt like days or even weeks pacing back and forth in that room, screaming at the walls and trying to find things he could break in fits of rage, which was impossible, as the tables and chairs were bolted to the floor, and even the magazines were petrified objects that could not be detached from the surfaces they lay on. It was torment. He who had made a career of *taking* people now couldn't even *take* objects.

He might have gone mad with frustration, but then, he'd always been mad, so there wouldn't have been much of a difference.

Then, after what seemed like forever, a familiar voice came through the loudspeaker on the wall. "Hello? Can you hear me?"

The People Taker recognized the soft and elegant voice as belonging to a beautiful if evil shadow named Ursula, who last he heard had been eaten by some kind of dinosaur.

He almost hurled himself at the speaker in desperation. "Yesssss, I can hhhhhear you! Are you imprisssssoned here, too?"

Her laugh was soft, musical, lovely, and completely vicious. "That's cute. No, Mr. People Taker, you're in a place built for prisoners of flesh and blood. That would prove no prison for one made of what I'm made of. I was more appropriately returned to my cell in the Hall of Shadow Criminals."

The People Taker felt an emotion that was normally utterly alien to him: embarrassment at having said something stupid. "Oh."

"The good news, darling, is that I am no longer a prisoner there, either. Our dark master, Lord Obsidian, was generous enough to send another army of his faceless shadows to smash the cells and free any who would agree to serve him. Of the entire population of that terrible prison, only one, Hieronymus Spector, foolishly refused our master's offer; the rest are free and either on their way to the Dark Country to join Obsidian's army, or here with me, to speak with you."

The People Taker jumped up and down in excitement. "Then fffffree me, curse you! I nnnnneed to get my hands on the What brats!"

The People Taker was not the most gracious of losers.

Ursula cooed, "I'm afraid I have to tell you that Gustav and the What girls and their father and their cat are all already down in the Dark Country and beyond our reach. Lord Obsidian sends word that he has plans for all of them that no longer require us."

The People Taker cursed at this news. He had made such wonderfully nasty plans for Gustav and Fernie and Pearlie and their father and that wretched cat.

"However," Ursula continued, "our liege still needs a flesh-and-blood ally to capture the fourth and final member of the What family. He is therefore still willing to employ you, if you are willing to risk facing the awful consequences of failing him a third time."

"Yesssss! Anything! Just fffffreeeee me!"

"Very well," said Ursula.

The door to his right clicked open.

The grand parlor of the Gloom mansion had changed since the last time the People Taker had seen it. He knew that a number of the staircases linking some of the higher floors had collapsed during his last attempt to capture the What family, burying the floor and much of the fine furniture under twisted rubble. The wreckage had been cleared, the dust had been swept, and much of the damage had either been repaired or allowed to heal in the bizarre manner that this house always seemed to regenerate from its regular catastrophes, but the throngs of shadowy residents who were always visible mingling in the parlor, whatever else might have been happening around them, were now absent, having fled to their hiding places rather than spend any time around the sinister army gathered for Lord Obsidian's glory.

There must have been many hundreds of shadows, from the faceless shadow warriors who had just come up from the Dark Country, to the convicts they had freed from the Hall of Shadow Criminals. Most of the shadow warriors were faceless things without obvious personalities. The shadow criminals were all versions of recognizable human types, from the beautiful Ursula to the rather stupid Otis to snarling, leering, and scowling villains of every other type, some of whom had already made it clear to the People Taker that they didn't appreciate having to work with a "warm" like him.

The leader of the gang known as the Four Terrors, Nebuchadnezzar, was not present; according to Ursula, he had last been seen heading for the Dark Country and was probably still trying to catch Gustav and the What girls himself. That was okay, she said. Among the shadows in the room now were some of the greatest nightmares that the human or shadow world had ever known, and they would be more than up to any challenge.

Ursula addressed the crowd: "The mother of Fernie and Pearlie What, Nora What, is a professional adventurer. She travels all over the world of light confronting challenges for something the humans call television."

"Never heard of such a thing," said one of the

shadow criminals, a thug with one missing eye and a bulging jaw and forehead. "Hate it just on general principle."

The gathered shadow criminals nodded and murmured to one another, agreeing that whatever the strange television thing was, it was human and therefore worth hating.

"Many people do, apparently. It's only important to know that this strange job keeps her away from home for weeks or months at a time. Our spotters in the house's east tower reported seeing one of the human vehicles dropping her off at her home earlier today. It should not be long before she comes knocking here to try to find her family. When she does, it will be the People Taker's job to answer the door and lure her inside . . . so that we may swarm and capture her, take her to the Pit, and deliver her into our master's clutches."

The gathered shadow criminals nodded and murmured some more, liking any plan that involved throwing a human being into a bottomless pit.

In their midst, the People Taker snarled. He was not happy. He had until recently been one of Lord Obsidian's most valued servants, trusted with the command of monsters like the Beast, and assassins like the Four Terrors. Now, diminished by his failures, he was seen as no more than a messenger boy, fit only to open doors and play his role. He swore to himself that he would not be defeated this time. He promised that when this Nora What knocked on the door, he would not just play his role perfectly, but would also make her pay in the most terrible fashion for all the humiliations he had suffered at the hands of her simpering daughters.

The knock on the mansion's massive front doors echoed throughout the grand parlor.

"That will be her," said Ursula. "Play your role, dear. And this time, try not to mess up."

The People Taker grimaced again, nodded to indicate his understanding of the one menial role left to him, and headed into the entrance hall. As he went, he tamed his fierce, evil expression, and took on a gentle and unthreatening look to match the role he would wear to disguise his true intentions: that of Brad Gloom, a kind and gentle and neighborly man, who wouldn't dream of hurting anybody, not even a fly. But inside he thought of his favorite activity in all the world: *taking*.

He thought, *I'm coming to take you, Nora What.*

This time there will be no escape for a member of your family.

This time, even if you prove to be as dangerous as your daughters, even if you prove able to evade me, you will also have an army of shadows to contend with. You will not escape. Lord Obsidian will have you, and I will have the pleasure of knowing I took at least one of you.

You are doomed.

He used up the last of his snickers and opened the door.

CHAPTER TWO
THE FATE WORSE THAN DEATH DELUXE

Since first meeting her strange friend Gustav Gloom, Fernie What had spent more time fighting monsters and fleeing dinosaurs and traveling through time and space than the vast majority of other children her age, but she was still only ten years old, and that meant there were still any number of activities on her want list that she had never had a chance to try for herself.

For instance, she'd never ridden a grizzly bear, she'd never driven a submarine, she'd never played tennis on the wings of an airplane in flight, and she'd never eaten chocolate-covered grasshoppers.

Other unusual experiences were not on her want list.

She had never once wanted to be prodded along a narrow catwalk by the evil minions of a world-conquering villain as she was brought back to his castle as a prisoner.

That had never been among her plans.

But that was the situation she found herself in now.

Behind her, her guard said, "Careful, you."

He said this because the catwalk was only a couple of feet across, only wide enough for Fernie and her fellow captives to traverse it in single file. There were no safety railings to prevent a terrible fall, an omission that must have upset Fernie's safety-expert father very much when he'd been brought as a prisoner to the same castle some time ago. He was famous for always wanting safety railings on everything.

Fernie needed to concentrate on putting one foot in front of the other and keeping her balance, but couldn't resist asking her guard, "Why would you warn me to be careful? I'm just a prisoner, right?"

"That's true," the guard said.

"Then why would you care if I fell over the side and died?"

"I wouldn't," the guard said, "but this is my one job, and I like to be good at it. So hurry along."

"Which do you want me to do? *Be careful* or *hurry along*? I can't do both."

The guard hesitated. "You're right."

"So what do you want me to do?"

"Be careful hurrying along," the guard suggested, "and don't give me any more lip about it, or I'll just pitch you over the edge and take the poor performance review."

Fernie didn't want to be pitched over the side and take what would have been a lethal fall into the courtyard a couple of hundred feet below, so she did what the guard ordered and *was careful hurrying along*.

This was precisely the kind of thing she supposed she had to accept as the first in a long line of prisoners who had just been brought to this castle and were each now being escorted across the narrow catwalk by their own personal guard.

Despite the warning to be careful, she glanced over her shoulder, through the hulking and transparent gray form of her guard, to the form behind him, her twelve-year-old sister, Pearlie. Pearlie was more unsteady on the catwalk than Fernie was and had to extend both her arms for balance.

Behind Pearlie was another shadow guard, grim-faced and big-jawed and glowering so nastily that he might have been trying to set fire to something with the heat of his gaze.

Behind him was the pale, serious form of Fernie's best friend, Gustav Gloom, looking as always oddly calm and composed despite being surrounded by hostile enemies on all sides. Behind him marched another shadow guard, this one a woman with long stringy hair and eyes that looked more like boreholes some rodent had dug in a piece of wood.

Behind that guard was a burly, bearded innkeeper whom Gustav and the What girls had recently met, a longtime human resident who had been cut off from the world of light for so long that he'd forgotten his name, and for convenience's sake called himself Not-Roger.

That was about as far back in the line as Fernie could see at the moment, but she knew there'd be other prisoners back there, including a number of shadow allies: the beautiful Anemone, the mysterious hooded Caliban, and Not-Roger's own shadow (who couldn't remember Not-Roger's real name, either).

Farther back, there were even more prisoners, shadow and human, whom Fernie hadn't met, all of whom were being marched from the slave hold of the same zippalin that had captured Fernie and her friends.

This struck Fernie as a pretty crowded haul of prisoners, as such things went, but she gathered it wasn't any larger a collection than the guards of Lord Obsidian's castle were used to, as none of the ones prodding the group along seemed to be particularly impressed.

"Hey," Fernie's guard said. "I thought I told you to hurry along."

"Sorry," said Fernie. "I'm just checking on my sister and the rest of my friends."

"You're the prisoner of Lord Obsidian now. You're not allowed sisters or friends. If you're smart, you'll just do what you're ordered to do and look out for what's going to happen to you if you don't."

Fernie said, "Okay, but since I've already been told that falling into Lord Obsidian's hands is a Fate Worse Than Death, all by itself, just how much worse could the punishment for not hurrying along be? Is it, like, The Fate Even Worse Than The Fate Worse Than Death? Or The Fate Worse Than Death Deluxe?"

"That does it," said the guard. "You're in real trouble now. I'm going to report your attitude to the boss."

"Gee," said Fernie. "And here I was, doing so well up until this point."

15

The guard prodded her with his spear-point, not enough to draw blood but enough to suggest that he'd only let her get away with as much mockery as he was willing to take.

Fernie shrugged and went back to carefully hurrying along.

All in all, she considered this far from the most fun she'd ever had. The Dark Country was a gray and dreary place to begin with, and the ebony castle of Lord Obsidian was not much improved for being the first halfway-civilized place she'd encountered since her arrival. It was just a collection of shadowy gray towers connected by great stone walls that separated the grounds into what amounted to open pens.

The towers and walls numbered in the dozens, all rising high above a deep churning gray mist that looked pretty much the same on all sides of the separating walls. The only real detail to the landscape was a pair of suspiciously round black mountains dominating the horizon to Fernie's right, each of them rising so high into the sky that their peaks were lost in the clouds above. Something about those mountains looked familiar, but her mind refused to identify exactly how. She had the idea that it was sparing her the moment of recognition because she had too much else to worry about right now.

Looking straight down at the misty courtyard below her wasn't much better. From time to time it came into focus as a sea of forlorn shadow-faces moaning about the hopelessness of their lot.

Fernie risked another question. "Who are they?"

"More prisoners," the guard behind her explained. "Enemies of the great Obsidian. The shadows who tried to resist him are even worse off, being captured by him, than you human types are. He uses them, he does."

Had Fernie not already possessed good reason to consider Gustav Gloom's enemy Lord Obsidian a real creep, the sight of all those despairing shadows would have provided her with a fine first clue. It wasn't the kind of sight nice people preferred to see from their castles. It was the kind of sight awful people used to remind themselves of all the unhappiness they'd caused. Only a real villain wanted to look out his window and see that kind of thing before breakfast.

Up ahead, the catwalk ended at an ominous stone tower studded with balconies from which many armored shadow minions shouted nasty things at the prisoners being brought toward them. Unlike most of the shadows Fernie and Pearlie and Gustav had seen so far—who, like their fellow prisoners Anemone and Caliban and Not-Roger's shadow, had all tended to look pretty human—these had taken on more monstrous shapes, almost as if it would not have been enough for them to just look like bad people; they had to look like things worse than people, or things that ate people.

"'Ey!" said one whose mouth sported a pair of walrus tusks. "Look over there! I'll sell me nose if that's not Gustav Gloom!"

An apelike figure cried, "The master will be 'appy about this, 'e will, 'e will. 'E's been ranting about Gustav Gloom for a while now!"

"Aye, 'e has such plans for the boy . . . !"

". . . And who's that red-haired little girl walking along in front of them? Not the little one with the curls . . . the taller one! That must be the other one the master wants: Fernie What!"

Behind Fernie, Pearlie cried out, "Shows how much you know, you big dummies! I'm not Fernie! I'm her bigger and tougher sister!"

"Oi! You hear that?"

"I did, I did! There's a tougher sister!"

"Won't do either one of 'em any good! It

won't, it won't! They'll both lose what toughness they have slaving in Lord Obsidian's mines!"

"It's just interesting that there's a tougher sister, that's all!"

"She don't look so bloomin' tough now! None of 'em do! Lookit them, all prisoners being led to a fate worse than death!"

The catwalk ended at a platform with a massive door overseen by an elderly, robed shadow whose eyebrows were so long at the sides that they joined his bushy mustache and beard in drooping all the way to the floor. He peered over his foggy bifocals at the four human beings who were the first of his prisoners, and said, "All right, all right, everybody, pipe down. This lot still has to be processed. Please line them up in front of me, will you? The three children over there, and that big bearded fellow . . . Yes, that's right. Him. Excellent."

Now that they were standing side by side, Fernie reached for Gustav's hand. He took hers and squeezed, a grip that betrayed no particular fear of the horrors they now faced. She glanced over and confirmed that he was holding Pearlie's hand as well, and that Pearlie was doing the same for the comically huge Not-Roger.

The shadow in the bifocals rolled back one page

of the stack of papers on his clipboard and read his next words from something printed there, rushing through the text in a monotone, as if he'd delivered this speech so many times that it had ceased to have any meaning for him. *"Be grateful, insignificant worms. Your puny lives are now the property of the all-wise, all-powerful Lord Obsidian, conqueror of the shadow realm and future destroyer of the world of light. Any complaints you might have about your treatment after you pass through this door should be kept to yourselves, as nobody who will be placed in charge of you cares. If you wish to survive, just remember this one thing: that if you disobey us in any way, it can always get much worse."*

He rolled the top sheet back, adjusted his bifocals, and said, "Right. So let's get to it. My name is Scrofulous, and it's my solemn duty to decide just which fate worse than death, out of all the many options provided to us by our lord and master, you will come to suffer from now until the end of time."

"Sounds like a fun job," said Fernie.

"Why, yes, it is. Please cooperate, and this can be a brief and convenient experience for all of us." He flipped the papers again and said, "Right. I'm told that one of you is the boy Gustav Gloom?"

Gustav Gloom released the hands of the What

sisters so he could step forward and jab a proud thumb at his chest. "I'm Gustav Gloom."

"Would you be the Gustav Gloom who's also the son of Hans and the grandson of Lemuel?"

"That's me," Gustav confirmed.

Scrofulous peered through the bifocals that enlarged his eyes and made them look as big as dinner plates. "Do you have any identification attesting to that, young man?"

"Sorry, no. I guess you'll have to let me go."

Scrofulous spent the next few seconds blinking, as if this was an option that had never been mentioned to him before and he had to give it careful consideration before rejecting it out of hand. Then he coughed and said, "Ah, I see. A joke. We don't have those here. Our lord and master has declared them illegal. In any event, I do suppose it's safe enough to assume that you are who you say you are, since this is Lord Obsidian's place of power, and nobody with even an ounce of self-preservation would claim to be the son of his greatest enemy, unless he was. Our lord has been quite clear in his daily, crazed, inspirational rants that you were to be delivered to him the instant you were captured. So you, at least, we've got sorted out."

Gustav shook his head and said, "Sorry. But no."

CHAPTER THREE
MAKING SCROFULOUS'S JOB DIFFICULT

Scrofulous flipped through the papers on his clipboard, searching for the proper response to such an outrage, found none, and replied, "Excuse me, young man. Did you just say *No*?"

"Yes."

"Ah," said Scrofulous, his eyebrows lowering like a pair of curtains. "You realized your mistake and have now decided to say *Yes* instead."

"It wasn't a mistake," Gustav explained. "I'm just answering your most recent question this time. You asked me if I had said *No*, and I had, so I said *Yes*."

"Was that first *No* a *No* as in, *No, please, anything but that, I beg you, no?*"

"It was *No* as in, *I didn't come here to waste time with Lord Obsidian. I came here to find and rescue my father, Hans, who I've been led to believe you're holding prisoner. It's No as in, You will bring me to see him, Scrofulous, or you will be very sorry you didn't, the next time we meet.*"

This must have been an entirely new experience for Scrofulous, the gatekeeper at this place that was supposed to be entirely without hope: not just defiance, but defiance backed up with threats. He drummed his fingers on his clipboard. "You know, I almost believe you."

"You should try a little harder," Gustav suggested.

"I admire your confidence. Alas, you're not the first prisoner dragged before Lord Obsidian, and in my experience the defiant ones generally don't tend to survive long enough to carry out any brave threats. So that settles that."

"I disagree," said Gustav, with unshakeable calm, "but feel free to use your best judgment. We'll see who's right before long."

"Yes, well." Scrofulous ruffled through his papers. "It's Lord Obsidian's throne room for you. You can step back now."

Gustav obliged, though clearly less out of fear than politeness. He nodded at Fernie as he did, and she took a moment's comfort in the confidence he showed her; confidence that might have been misplaced, given how dire their situation was, but confidence that still hadn't been shaken by anything he'd been through so far. It was the kind of look that made her promise herself she wouldn't show any more fear than he just had.

Before her, Scrofulous ruffled papers. "So, next I'm told that we have your almost-as-infamous companion, Fernie What. That's an odd name."

"Says the guy called Scrofulous," muttered Fernie.

"Be quiet, girl. I haven't gotten to you yet. I want this dangerous renegade Fernie What . . . and since you're clearly too young to be such a feared creature, she must be that somewhat larger girl standing next to you." He turned to Pearlie. "Step forward, Fernie What."

Though taken aback at being the target of Scrofulous's pointing finger, Pearlie didn't move. "I'm not Fernie. I'm her older and even tougher sister, Pearlie."

Fernie gave her older sister an irritated glance. "Will you please stop telling everybody we meet in the Dark Country that you're tougher than me? It doesn't help."

"Maybe not," Pearlie said implacably, "but it's true."

Scrofulous rapped on his clipboard, hard. "Ladies, ladies! I don't care which one of you is tougher; I only care which one of you is Fernie. Will Fernie please step forward?"

Fernie took a giant step forward, clasped her hands behind her back, and stood at attention, which was exactly the roll-call position preferred by the gym teacher at her last school. "Present."

"You're Fernie What? Are you sure?"

"Last I checked," said Fernie.

"But you're the smaller one. Do you have any identification?"

"My dad sewed a name tag in the back of my shirt collar, and you can have somebody look at that if you want, but, really: Why would I pretend to be Fernie What, in this situation, if I wasn't?"

"An excellent point," said Scrofulous. He ruffled papers. "I believe I have you down for 'to be imprisoned in darkness while awaiting Obsidian's judgment.' You'll be taken to a suitably uncomfortable place to wait until our master decides what to do with you."

Fernie said, "No."

"Again, *No*?"

"That's right," Fernie said, "and again, it's

not *No* as in, *No, oh please, anything but that, show mercy, no*. It's *No, I came here to find my father, too, and I'm not letting you take me anywhere unless I get to see him.*"

Scrofulous drew back his clipboard as if preparing to throw it at someone. "Does *everybody* in the line today have a father they insist on seeing?"

Pearlie raised her right hand. "I do, but Fernie's father is my father, too, so you only have to make one trip between us."

"Don't forget mine while you're at it," Gustav prodded.

The man known as Not-Roger timidly raised his hand. "And, ummm . . ."

Scrofulous whirled. "Don't tell me *you* have a father in the dungeon!"

"I honestly can't swear that I do," confessed Not-Roger, "because I've been trapped in the Dark Country for so long that I no longer remember my real name or my family or for that matter much else about my life back in the world of light. But as long as you're retrieving everybody's fathers, I figure you might as well see if you have one of mine anywhere in your collection."

"That's a good idea," said Fernie. "As long as

27

you're gonna get two fathers, you might as well try for three. We'll wait."

By now poor Scrofulous was downright bouncing with indignation. "So let me get this straight. I'm not *just* expected to reunite our prisoners with their *actual* fathers, but also, while I'm at it, with any *hypothetical* fathers who we *might not even have* in the first place?"

"If it's not too much trouble," ventured Not-Roger.

"You can start with the ones you're sure about," suggested Gustav.

This was just about the last straw for Scrofulous, whose eyebrows had knit so violently by this point that they looked like a pair of wooly snakes meeting face-to-face to decide which one was going to eat the other. "Ravager! Take the boy to his meeting with our father in darkness, Lord Obsidian! Gnulbotz! Take Fernie What to the Screaming Room! Krawg and Hissfang! Take Pearlie What and the big oaf next to her to the Dungeon of Those Who Await!! Now bring forward the next prisoners, and get these insolent newcomers out of my sight!"

A quartet of shadow guards who merited these unappetizing names stepped forward. In the instant before they tugged at the arms of their prisoners and separated them for what could very easily turn out to be all time, Gustav and the What sisters felt the magnitude of the dangers facing them and threw themselves into a hug so tight that if sincerity alone had been enough to lend it strength, no force on earth or in the Dark Country would have ever been able to tear it apart.

Fernie struggled to come up with a good-bye that could possibly be powerful enough for the occasion. "Gustav. Pearlie. I . . ."

"Don't worry," Gustav said, under his breath. "This won't take long."

Hope raised a lump in her throat. "Don't tell me you have a plan!"

"No plan," said Gustav. "Not even an idea. Just a couple of vague notions." Then a shadow-collar looped around his throat, and he was pulled backward by his personal guard, the one called Ravager.

Fernie cried, "No!" and tried to fight, but by then the shadow guard called Gnulbotz had collared her and pulled her away from her sister. He had the nastiest smile Fernie had ever seen. There were actual little worms sticking their heads out of each and every one of his teeth, and they waved those heads like dancing cobras. Fernie fought long enough to see Pearlie reaching for her, only to be pulled back and secured alongside the giant Not-Roger. Behind them both, a fresh set of prisoners—including the hooded shadow Caliban, the beautiful shadow Anemone, and Not-Roger's own shadow, identical to the man except that he could be seen through—were all being brought forward to be the next subjected to Scrofulous's clipboard.

Anemone had enough time to meet Fernie's despairing glance with her own . . . and for a moment her beautiful features slipped, revealing the older and more maternal features of the shadow Fernie had known as Gustav's great-aunt Mellifluous.

Fernie had already figured out that Anemone was Great-Aunt Mellifluous in disguise, but didn't have enough time to read much of use in the old woman's expression before being pulled away. Was Mellifluous despairing, too? Or afraid? Or ashamed of letting things get this far? Or was there a secret smile there, something to give Fernie hope as she was brought to whatever terrible place Lord Obsidian intended for her?

Leading a squad of other shadow guards, Gnulbotz marched her through a stone archway and into a tunnel of jagged walls and stalactite ceilings, where a gallery of lost prisoners cried out for mercy behind barred windows.

Gnulbotz's laugh was terrible even by the standard of cruel laughs, mostly because his wasn't the only voice laughing; somehow, when he cackled, a small chorus of smaller and squeakier cackles, probably the worms inhabiting his teeth, cackled along with him. "You're an unlucky one, aren't you? Not as unlucky as your friend in the black suit who'll have to face the terrible one himself . . . but unlucky enough to be headed where you're going."

Fernie remembered the name of the chamber she'd been condemned to. "What's so terrible about the Screaming Room?"

"It's the place our lord banished the only being he ever truly feared—a place where he has also chained hundreds of shadows driven insane by his treatment of them. It is said that even the strongest grown man cannot spend more than a day chained in their presence, trapped in darkness listening to the awful sounds they never stop making, without losing his mind forever . . . and I wager that the mind of a mere child such as yourself won't long outlast the echo of the slamming trapdoor."

Fernie felt true terror for the first time since her arrival in the Dark Country, but her mind was still racing. "The only human being Lord Obsidian ever feared . . . that would be my friend Gustav's father, right? That would be . . . Hans Gloom?"

"Aye, so it was . . . but if you're thinking there's any help to be had from him, you can think again. From what I hear, he lost his mind only a short time after Lord Obsidian locked him up in that terrible place. He's got the brain of a turnip now, and you, my dear, are about to join him." He cackled again, the worms cackling with him. "You shouldn't have made such a big deal about finding fathers, girl. If you hadn't mentioned it, Scrofulous might have been satisfied with just putting you in the same dungeon as your sister."

She tried to run then, but the collar pulled her up short, and all her useless attempt at escape accomplished was getting Gnulbotz to tighten his grip on her leash.

The sights and sounds of Obsidian's castle grew worse and worse, the deeper her guard led her into the castle. She saw things so awful that she found herself thinking her mind wouldn't last long enough to be shattered in the Screaming Room. But every time she felt herself start to break, she shut her eyes and thought of everybody depending on her: of her father, the safety expert who had envisioned so many of the world's hidden dangers but never considered the ones that came from the Dark Country; of her mother, the professional adventurer, who had braved so many dangers but would not be ready for the empty house she would find when she returned from her latest expedition; of Pearlie, who was pretty tough but (Fernie knew) not tough enough to get through this without a little sister to help her; of her best and truest friend, Gustav Gloom, who would be so alone without her if she did not live through this; and of even her cat, Harrington, who last she'd seen was being cared for on the Cryptic Carousel by the shadow of Gustav's grandfather Lemuel. Being a cat, Harrington was sometimes reserved with the love he gave, but he had never once allowed a minute's confusion about the amount of love he needed. They all counted on Fernie to get through whatever horror faced her with her mind and her courage intact.

But Gnulbotz had to ruin that just as they stopped before a grate in the floor. "I know what you're doing," he said. "You're gathering up all your courage. Giving yourself a rousing speech, in the hope that it will be enough. Am I right?"

She wanted to retort that it was none of his business. But all of a sudden she was too scared to come up with a defiant line. She could only watch as he lifted up the grate and revealed a bottomless black hole, from which the sound of distant wailing could be heard. She gulped, and answered, "Y-yes."

Gnulbotz removed the collar from around her neck and gave her a little affectionate pat on the shoulder. "Poor girl. It won't be even close to enough. You won't even last a minute, chained among their lot. Here, now, let me get what you'll be wearing from now on."

One of the other guards in Gnulbotz's squad handed him the chains that he would use to bind her—terrible barbed things, designed to hurt as well as confine, with rings for her neck, wrists, and ankles. Fernie knew she could never hope to escape, not even if she wore them for a hundred years.

The sounds from the opening in the floor

were awful—so awful that she could feel her sanity already wavering—even from up where she was. She hated the idea of entering that terrible place. But with Gnulbotz keeping a close eye on her to make sure she didn't run, the guards surrounding her on all sides, and her only other choice being tossed into that hole with the added handicap of chains, she did the only thing that offered her even the slightest taste of hope.

"No, thank you," she said, "I'll do without," and jumped in before he could stop her.

CHAPTER FOUR
WHAT GUSTAV FINDS IN THE THRONE ROOM OF LORD OBSIDIAN

Leading his own squadron of silent guards, the evil shadow named Ravager emitted loud rippling noises, and a number of unpleasant odors, all the way through what seemed like many confusing miles of corridors and stairways, to the highest regions of Lord Obsidian's castle.

It was almost a relief by the time they arrived at a set of black double doors carved with thorns and guarded on either side by shadow soldiers with swirling darkness instead of faces. Without a word, the soldiers opened the doors, revealing a room so shrouded in mist that even Gustav, whose eyes had been able to make out the details of the Dark Country even as he looked down at that cloud-covered landscape from a height, was unable to discern what terrors waited within.

Ravager removed Gustav's collar and leash and said, "In you go."

"Really?" Gustav asked. "I expected you to escort me in under guard."

The soldier to the right of the door rumbled his reply in a voice like the crash of angry thunder. "ALL PRISONERS BROUGHT HERE MUST ENTER LORD OBSIDIAN'S PRESENCE UNDER THEIR OWN POWER. THEY MUST BE ALONE WHEN FIRST THEY FACE HIM."

"I see." Gustav nodded. "He must be too much of a coward to deal with larger groups."

"DO NOT SPEAK ILL OF OUR MASTER OR YOU WILL BE PUNISHED."

Gustav almost laughed at that, but instead nodded again and did what the soldiers required of him.

Judging from the sound of his footsteps on the ebony stone echoing against the distant walls and ceiling, the chamber must have been the size of a stadium.

Gustav knew from his experiences in the house where he'd spent all his life that certain places can take on the flavors of the events that have happened there, becoming happy or sad or otherwise haunted by the experiences of those who knew those places well. For instance, the Hall of Shadow Criminals, back at his own house, was a place that felt like the despair of the beings imprisoned within. By contrast, he had always imagined that the Fluorescent Salmon home belonging to the Whats must have possessed the special kind of life that only energizes the homes of happy and loving families. This all made sense to him . . . but this place felt cold, malignant, evil, as if all warmth had fled to get away from an occupant who could only have done what he'd done if he hated everything that lived.

A voice like breaking glass said, "That is far enough."

Gustav obeyed. "Am I talking to Howard Philip October?"

"That was once my human name. It was what I called myself before I transformed into something all-powerful, pitiless, grotesque, and terrifying, something that could only be called Lord Obsidian."

"Something," Gustav noted, "that likes to talk about itself, and also has terrible taste in names."

"If you value your life, you will show me enough respect to address me by the title I have assumed now, the title of a creature beyond the paltry imagination of a child."

"A bully, a murderer, and a liar . . . Howie."

"Very well. We have been so vital to each other that there should be no pretenses between us. You may advance, and admire the sculpture gallery of my life."

The mists retreated, revealing one small bit at a time.

The first furnishing to be revealed was the statue of a little boy with golden curls, dressed in a sailor outfit and clutching an ice-cream sandwich.

"Myself," said Lord Obsidian. "Pampered child of a family well known for the fortune it made peddling children's treats. I was so innocent that my aunt Louise called me 'Little Sunshine.' At no moment during my formative years was I ever allowed to doubt that I was destined for greatness."

"So this is all about you being a spoiled brat?"

The mists retreated again, revealing a larger statue of Howard Philip October as a young adult, dressed in a tweedy old jacket and peering at the world with a bland long face dominated by an oversize forehead and chin.

"Myself as a student of metaphysics, at the time of life when I quickly learned that my teachers were fools who only saw the surface of things, and never what lay beneath. I was so brilliant, even then, that my fellow students grew to fear me, and learned to cross the street whenever they saw me approaching."

"I can think of another explanation for that, Howie."

The mists retreated again to reveal another statue of an older Howard Philip October seated at an antique rolltop desk.

"Myself as an accomplished, if underappreciated, scholar attempting to educate the world about the shadowy forces that lay beneath the world they knew. Here, I am shown writing a letter to your accursed grandfather Lemuel, who had made some small discoveries of his own. I offered the fruits of my own genius to guide his poor, overrated research into more profitable directions. He should not have said no to me, young Gustav. I have made many suffer for his disrespect."

"You grew up a brat, Howie," Gustav translated, "and you remained a brat."

The mists drew back again and this time revealed a statue from a part of Lord Obsidian's life that Gustav had only learned about recently: the moment after years in the Dark Country when Howard Philip October had shed his human skin like an old garment and emerged as the shadow who would become known as Lord Obsidian. The statue depicted an indistinct, blurred, but somehow still terrible figure emerging from what looked like a wrinkled sack piled up at his ankles.

"The glorious moment when I became what I am."

"And lost everything you should have worked harder to keep," Gustav replied.

The mists retreated one last time and finally revealed Lord Obsidian on his throne.

The throne had the texture of polished glass but seemed to be an aquarium of sorts, only filled with inky shadow-stuff instead of water. Pale and distraught faces drifted in and out of the mists, becoming visible only long enough to open their mouths in terrified screams before clutching hands pulled them back. The wall behind the throne was made of the same kind of glass, and other shadow prisoners drifted to and fro behind it, as well, some of them reaching for Gustav as if they thought he could save them.

Lord Obsidian was the size of a small house. He was shaped more or less like the man he'd once been, but the already-long face had grown longer, curving at top and bottom to form a crescent moon with sharp points at the chin and forehead. He was made of something so dark, even by the standard of this country where all shadows came from, that it was difficult to make out all his details, but his limbs were as long as trees and had a couple of extra knees or elbows apiece. The clawed fingers curling over the edges of the throne's massive armrests were long enough to extend all the way to the stone floor.

One of his impossibly long hands drifted to the side of the throne and stroked a cloud of churning darkness that waited there like an obedient pet.

Gustav's heart sank at the sight of that pet. He'd fled it and fought it back when it served another enemy of his, the killer known only as the People Taker. It was every shapeless shadow that had ever been mistaken for a horrible monster, in every darkened bedroom of every child.

Gustav had hoped to never see it again, but here it was, at the side of its true master.

It had no real name. It was only called the Beast.

Lord Obsidian shifted position on his throne, his lanky arms and legs folding and unfolding in ways that no human skeleton would have managed without serious injury. "Now you see me, boy. This is how I have been remade by this shadowed world into which you have blundered. Do you still think that I should be insulted by your foolish reminders that I once wore the name of a mere man?"

"You should be insulted in some way, Howie,

but I haven't figured out all the best words yet."

The figure on the throne snarled, and scraped his sharp fingernails against the stone at his feet, striking sparks. "Who do you believe you are, to speak to me in such a disrespectful fashion?"

"Who am *I*?" Gustav repeated, in the manner of a boy who had never in his life heard such a stupid question. "You *know* who I am. I'm Gustav Gloom. Grandson of Lemuel Gloom. Son of—"

A finger-joint as long as a yardstick, ending with one dagger of a claw, slashed through the air and pressed painfully into the tip of Gustav's nose.

"You honestly don't need to go through the whole list," Lord Obsidian chided. "Your hated father, Hans, also had a habit of making windy speeches like that, back when he was chasing me across the dark lands. Spare us that and the boring recitation of your grievances against me, and we can move on to more profitable subjects."

The claw withdrew.

Beside him, the Beast stirred, yawned, then stiffened, its eyeless face registering the presence of the boy it had fought before.

Gustav repeated, "More *profitable* subjects."

"Yes."

"You think I came all this way to make a *deal* with you?"

"No. But now that you are here, you must know that you stand no chance against me. You must realize that you'll be better off choosing this moment to negotiate the terms of your surrender."

"You mean, like giving myself up in exchange for the lives of my friends?"

"No. That might have worked if we had made this deal while you were still within the confines of your house. But that was before you and the What girls defeated my People Taker, before you humiliated my Beast, before you prevented my agent from bringing me that wonderful treasure, the Nightmare Vault. That was before you declared war on me and foolishly allowed yourself to be captured. Now, if only to preserve my own dignity, you need to be punished, and so your friends and your father will all be forever lost to you. You may well see them again, briefly, if only so I may show you what unimaginable torments they face because of you, but their freedom will remain the price you'll have to pay for your past acts of defiance."

Gustav felt something burning in his heart, something that had never ever burned in him with enough heat to scald him, and found himself thinking, as if from a great distance: *This must be how real hatred feels.* "Go on."

"Still, there are ways you may yet make your own personal situation better. You are, after all, a halfsie, part boy and part shadow. That makes you an unusual thing, and I can always use the services of unusual things. If you agree to serve me, and start by leading me to the Nightmare Vault, I can soon make you a prince of the new universe we'll build on the wreckage of the old."

This was very, very bad. Up until this moment, Gustav had hoped that Lord Obsidian had given up on obtaining the Nightmare Vault, which imprisoned the sleeping shadows of dangerous creatures from before time. They were shadows who, if ever awakened, would burst forth to devour everyone and everything, clearing ground so Lord Obsidian could replace the universe that got eaten with a universe closer to his own liking. It was hidden, but in too convenient a place, and if Lord Obsidian ever figured out where, nobody in the world of light would live to see another sunrise.

Gustav gulped. "That's some deal, Howie. You're asking me to betray my friends, family, and everybody I care about."

Lord Obsidian chuckled, with what sounded

like genuine affection. "Oh, Gustav. You would not lose anything you haven't already lost and were not going to lose anyway."

"That's a lie."

Lord Obsidian began to tick off a list on ebony fingers as long and as cutting as swords.

"Think: Your human mother, Penny, died before you were born.

"Her shadow abandoned you without explanation when you were five.

"Your father, Hans Gloom, fell into the Dark Country years ago, and has never been a part of your life. He does not even know that you exist.

"Most of the shadows of the Gloom house barely tolerated you and could not care less whether you lived or died.

"Your guardian, Mellifluous, cared about you so little that she left you alone when she joined the resistance battle against me.

"The two insipid What girls claimed to be your friends, but we both know that their cowardly father feared for their safety around you and was planning to take them away to some other home where you would never see them again. In the world of light, it would not have taken long for them to forget all about you. I assure you that as my prisoners, it will not take them long to learn to curse your name.

"Who else do you have? The cat Harrington? Do not make me laugh. As a man, I had cats. I know what they're like.

"Even the very world I am asking you to help me destroy is a place that has no claim on your affections, because it exists outside the gates of your estate, apart from the shadow magic that keeps you alive in the world of light. You have never known it. So you should not waste your energy missing it.

"These are all things that you should be prepared to give up, because they are all things that you never truly had.

"I, on the other hand, am offering you power and a place at my side. Think about it, and you will see that it is a much better deal."

Gustav's heart felt like a hammer beating against his ribs. "You're wrong about everything, Howie. Even cats."

"I once had friends and family in my life. I've since discovered that power is better."

"You had people who cared about you," Gustav replied, "not people you bothered to care about. As friends, you had my father and the woman who would have been my mother. I've seen the pictures, Howie. Until you betrayed them, they *liked* you. They considered you *family*. They loved you. But then you killed her and broke his heart. Was all the power that you earned worth everything you had to give up?"

Lord Obsidian tilted his giant crescent-shaped head, as if considering the question. Enough of his face came into focus to give Gustav his first glimpse of the monster's terrible eyes, narrowing in contempt. They were like coals. No soul, no warmth, and no human feeling hid behind them.

Lord Obsidian said, "We are not finished with this discussion, you and I. But for now, perhaps you need a reminder of who wields the power in this room."

He lifted his terrible hand off the churning ball of darkness at his side—a shape that immediately rose and shook itself like a junkyard dog awakening from its nap to attack the trespassers it has heard skulking on the wrong side of its fence.

"Beast?" Lord Obsidian said. "Cause this insolent boy some pain."

This was precisely the invitation the Beast had been waiting for.

It lowered its head and charged.

CHAPTER FIVE
WHAT FERNIE FINDS
IN THE SCREAMING ROOM

The five seconds following Fernie's plunge into the Screaming Room were the very worst of her life.

She didn't actually land anywhere, but during those five seconds she felt herself surrounded by weeping shadowy faces, all moaning how all hope was gone, and how lost and alone she would now be forever.

After three seconds she knew that Gnulbotz had been right. Chained or unchained, she would lose her mind here in no time at all.

This was why it was so surprising, two seconds later, when those bereft moans went away and she found herself lying on her back, blinking at a sun that didn't hurt her eyes at all.

It had the dull look the sun has when it's hidden behind fat clouds and is no longer painful to look at, just a slightly brighter spot in the sky, no harder to look at than a light fixture behind frosted glass.

It wasn't even as bright as it had been when she had seen this particular sun before.

It had hung from the ceiling in one of the strangest rooms she'd ever visited, the room inside Gustav Gloom's house that contained another, smaller house. The room had a ceiling painted to resemble blue sky, and walls painted to resemble farmland with cows and distant hills. At the center of it sat a rustic farmhouse, with a front porch and a screen door and a slanted roof and all the comforts a family could ever want.

Gustav's grandfather Lemuel had raised his son, Hans, in that house inside the house. Until the day Howard Philip October committed his terrible crimes against the Gloom family, Hans and Penelope Gloom had been planning to raise their own family in the same place.

Fernie turned her head and saw the fake grass of the house's fake lawn stretching out before her, with the house inside the house looking very much like it had the first time she'd seen it, without all the terrible damage it had also suffered on that terrible night. It unfortunately also seemed drearier, and more colorless, and in some ways less detailed than the house she had visited.

The sky above her was not blue, but gray. The sun above her was also gray, when it should have been burning yellow. The fake grass she lay on did not feel like fake grass, but more like cold stone, and if she listened very carefully, she could still hear the moaning and wailing shadows in the cell where she'd been tossed, not nearly as distant as she would have liked them to be, but just far enough that she didn't have to listen to them if she didn't want to.

This was too dreary a place to be the warm and inviting, if somewhat sad, chamber that Gustav had shown her. But it was very much like that place, or at least more like that place than it was like the Screaming Room she'd been threatened with.

She didn't for one second believe that this was what she'd been intended to find when she was thrown into the hole in the floor. This was something Scrofulous hadn't planned for . . . something that even Lord Obsidian hadn't planned for.

It didn't feel like a *rescue*. Not exactly.

But it was something *unexpected*, and she supposed that she could take some encouragement from that.

So she stood on shaky legs, faced the house, and said, "Hello?"

Nobody answered. But it was impossible to believe that she was alone here. There was a presence of some kind all around her—an interested, observing *something* that she could feel the same way it was sometimes possible to feel someone looking over her shoulder.

"Hello? Is there anybody there? Where is this place?"

Again, there was no answer.

Maybe the house in front of her harbored some unimaginable horror that would leap out at her as soon as she passed through the screen door into whatever room waited beyond it.

But there was nowhere else to go and nothing else for her to do, so she crossed the lawn, climbed the three creaky steps to the rustic porch, and passed through the screen door into the house beyond, still calling, "Hello?"

Inside, this version of the house looked exactly like the real one had the first time she'd seen it, except all gray, and missing much of the detail she had seen in her visit to the real place. It didn't feel the same and it didn't smell the same. When she crossed into the living room, similar to the one where she and Gustav had discussed what happened to his parents, it, too, looked a lot like the place she'd visited, complete with windows open to a painted backdrop of distant cows. But the details were as off on the inside as they were on the outside. When she examined the books on the shelves, she found one she remembered finding there before, *The Haunting of Hill House*, by Shirley Jackson. Gustav had said it was a great book. But when she took it off the shelf, it had no texture and weighed nothing in her hand. When she flipped the pages, she discovered them to be blank.

It was going to be boring, trapped here forever, if the books on the shelves had no words in them.

Fernie put the book down and turned to investigate the rest of the room, discovering that the couch was occupied by what looked like a great black storm cloud that seemed to gather some of its substance closer to itself as she approached. It had a vague face, less like a proper face than a cartoon with two dark patches for eyes and another for a mouth.

Fernie had seen a cloud like that before, on a distant world with red skies. The cloud had been a shadow, driven half mad by years of imprisonment, and had been quite dangerous indeed until brought to its senses.

She could only hope that she had as much luck with this one. "Hello."

The cloud rumbled like distant thunder just beginning to roll in over the hills. "Who are you?"

"M-my name's Fernie. Fernie What."

"That is just a name. It tells me nothing. Who are you, Fernie What?"

"I'm a girl from the world of light."

"You're also only a child, which is why I have gone to the trouble of shielding you from this chamber's madness. I wish no harm to children. But still, you have told me nothing."

"I'm sorry. I'll try to do better."

"Who are you, aside from a girl from the world of light?"

"I'm the daughter of Nora and Sidney What, and the sister of Pearlie What."

"Those names also mean nothing to me."

"I can't help that," said Fernie. "But they're my family. They mean everything to me."

The walls seemed to thin, and the distant wailing grew louder. It was a terrible sound, even when it was muffled, and for a second it grew so loud that Fernie almost started screaming herself. She caught a glimpse of what made that sound: hundreds of indistinct shapes, imprisoned by chains of what looked like black smoke, wailing in terrible madness. Then the walls of the house inside the house thickened again, the chained figures were once again lost to view, and the terrible sound of their suffering was distant background noise once more—something that could never be ignored, but could, for the moment, be endured.

"Family is important," the cloud said, finally.

Fernie became aware that she had fallen to her knees. "Yes. I know."

"Why are you not with your family, Fernie What?"

"They've been taken," Fernie said, and before the cloud could ask her another question, she quickly slipped in one of her own. "Am I still in the Screaming Room?"

"You are indeed still in that terrible place, Fernie What. But you are also inside of me, a shadow who came here willingly on an errand of mercy. Were it not for this illusion that I have made of my own substance, this shadowy stage set that I have created and brought you into, your mind would now be shattering from the terrible sounds of the shadows who scream without end in this place. So you depend on me for your sanity. But I will continue to protect you, as long as I confirm that you deserve my protection."

"But I've already told you my name and where I came from, even the names of my family. I don't know what else I can tell you."

"Then let me ask the questions. You have the smell of someone who's been in the Dark Country for a while, but I also sense sunshine not very far in your past. Tell me, child: How did you come to be brought to the Dark Country against your will?"

This, at least, was something Fernie could answer. "I didn't come here against my will. I came here on purpose, with my sister and my best friend in the whole world."

"Why would innocent children throw their lives away in such a foolish manner?"

Fernie said, "To rescue two good men."

"It doesn't appear to have been a very successful rescue."

"Not at the moment," Fernie admitted. "But I'm not willing to say it's failed yet."

"Why not?"

"Because the best friend I mentioned is the bravest and smartest person I've ever known.

Because he fights monsters and beats them. Because when he's asked to do something impossible, he shrugs and he blinks and he figures out a way to make it happen. Because when everything's at its worst, he's always at his best. Because he'll get us out of here. He will. Just you wait."

The cloud made a thrumming noise . . . which made no sense at all to Fernie until she thought of the sound people make while drumming their fingertips against a tabletop. It was thinking.

After long seconds, the cloud asked her what sounded like a very sad question: "Do you mistake this for a fairy tale, Fernie What? Are you just another foolish, empty-headed little girl who's read too many stories and puts too much faith in being rescued by some invincible hero?"

Fernie had the sense that the shadow-being before her had lost something very precious at some point in its past, and that everything rode on the answer she gave it.

"No. If I've learned anything at all since this whole mess started, it's that *I'm* a hero. I don't need to go looking for any. But even a hero can put her faith in a friend."

"He must be some friend, Fernie What."

"He is."

What followed was a dead silence, while the shadow creature figured out where next to take the interview. Fernie was afraid that once it started up again, the questions would keep going until she was forced to recount everything that had happened since the moment she first spotted Gustav through the iron fence that encircled his yard. So she asked another one of her own. "Why does this place look so much like the house where Hans and Penny Gloom lived?"

The cloud drew back. "You have already seen the house inside the house? How?"

"Gustav Gloom showed me. He's my best friend."

The cloud turned so dark in the next second or two that Fernie wondered if she'd just angered it in some way. "You . . . are Gustav's best friend? You are not lying to me? Gustav has a best friend from the world of light?"

"Yes. Of course he does."

The cloud trembled, though whether in fear, or rage, or madness, or some other emotion that only a shadow enduring imprisonment in this terrible place could feel, was something Fernie had no way of knowing.

"I didn't recognize you," it said. "You . . . You're the one from the painting."

Fernie had no idea what the cloud was talking about. "What painting?"

The cloud suddenly rolled off the couch, revealing what its presence had been hiding: the figure of a silver-haired man, a real man and not the shadow of a man, curled in sleep. She had barely a second to consider the only person he could possibly be, the long-missing Hans Gloom, before the cloud shadow was upon her, wrapping limbs of black smoke around her shoulders.

For a moment she was terribly afraid that by mentioning Gustav's name, she'd awoken a horrible enemy, in this place where Gustav had so many enemies.

But then she realized that the tendrils of smoke had just pulled themselves together to become arms, and that the indistinct cloud had just pulled itself into the shape of a pretty young woman whose face Fernie had seen in photographs and paintings.

"Oh, *thank you*," the shadow woman said, in a voice that no longer sounded like a distant storm cloud but now resembled the weeping of a young mother who'd been consumed by worry for far too long. "Thank you, thank you, thank you, Fernie."

"For what?"

"All these years trapped here I've been afraid that my beautiful boy, trapped *there*, in that house, behind that fence, would never find any friends to care for him. Thank you, thank you, thank you, Fernie, for being his friend and letting me know that he turned out the way he has."

Fernie pulled back and looked the shadow woman in the face. "I know you."

Fernie's new protector was indeed Penny's shadow, the one who had rescued an unborn child from the twisted wreckage that had taken the Penny of flesh and blood.

"Yes," she said. "I'm Gustav's mother."

CHAPTER SIX
WHAT PEARLIE AND NOT-ROGER FIND IN THE DUNGEON OF THOSE WHO AWAIT

Elsewhere, Not-Roger said, "I miss my shadow."

Pearlie What replied, "I miss mine, too."

"I know," he sighed, "but I suspect it's different for you. From what I gather, you've pretty much always had other people around you—your sister, your father, Gustav, any number of others. Your shadow was just something that followed you around and didn't speak up much. For a long time my shadow was the only friend I had, the only person I knew who I could do things with."

"Like what?"

"Well, you know that game I Spy?"

Pearlie happened to hate that game, but her dad insisted on playing it on long car trips. "Sure, you pick something you can see from where you are, and say, 'I spy, with my little eye, something starting with the letter . . .' and you say the letter the thing starts with. Then the person you're playing with has to figure out what you're thinking of."

"That's the game, all right," said Not-Roger. "We must have played that thousands of times during our years running the inn. Of course, it wasn't the most challenging game ever, because my shadow always picked the letter *S*, and the inn was such an empty place that the only things he could possibly be thinking of were other shadows."

The two of them had been imprisoned in the Dungeon of Those Who Await for about half an hour, as far as Pearlie could tell, and so far all she could say about it was that it was large and difficult to cross. This was because the floor in the dungeon was not flat, but was instead a strange arrangement of steps that sometimes headed up and sometimes headed down and sometimes forced travelers to walk up three steps, then down four, and then up another six, and then down another three, and up another twenty, just to get to some random high point that should have been only a short walk away in the first place.

Every surface was lined with shadows and

human beings who had given up on trying to get anywhere in this confusing place and now huddled wherever they'd happened to stop, gathered like thousands of visitors in the bleachers of a stadium where there was nothing to look at but others who, like them, had run out of hope.

It was impossible to imagine why anybody, even a world-conquering type like Lord Obsidian, would ever need so many prisoners, but Pearlie and Not-Roger had already asked that question of one of the hopeless figures they encountered, the shadow of a skinny old man with a beard that fell all the way to his ankles.

"I used to be one of his closest advisors," the bearded shadow had sighed. "Alas, I made the mistake of once—once!—advising him that perhaps he might be wrong about something. He saw this as an unacceptable moment of rebellion, and threw me in here, telling me that I would have to wait until he thought up something he could do to me that could possibly be terrible enough."

Pearlie had protested, "That can't be the same reason everybody's here!"

"Why not? Lord Obsidian probably doesn't

even remember one-tenth of all the human beings and shadows he's thrown in here for what he imagined to be the short time it would take him to think of some particularly vile fate to punish them with. And if you're one of them, girl, you might as well hope that nobody ever reminds him of you. This place, awful as it is, is much better than anything he could ever come up with."

This taught Pearlie and Not-Roger nothing except what they already knew: that Lord Obsidian was a terrible person.

"Why is he so mean?" Pearlie asked aloud. It was the same question she and Fernie had asked a number of times, in a number of ways, since first learning of Lord Obsidian's existence. "What exactly does he think he's getting out of it? What does he think he's winning?"

Not-Roger shook his head. "Ah, girl. I seem to remember people asking those questions about any number of bullies and villains, before I got banished from the world of light. As I told you, I wasn't a very nice man when I lived there, and they were asked more than once of me."

Pearlie had not found out exactly what Not-Roger meant when he said he hadn't been a very nice man, though lies and thievery seemed to have been somehow involved. "Well, maybe you can answer me, then. What did *you* get out of it?"

"I don't remember, exactly. It's been such a long time, after all. But I seem to recall that I never really thought I was winning the game of life unless somebody else was losing. After a while, being happy and making other people unhappy was all mixed up in my head, and I tended to think that one was the same as the other."

They climbed to the top of one pyramid of steps, where the wheezing Not-Roger, exhausted by all this hiking, had to sit down and rest. Pearlie looked out upon the throngs, and for a few moments felt despair and loneliness wash over her like a wave.

"I was hoping to find my dad here, but I don't see him anywhere."

Not-Roger said, "Try looking for your house keys."

"My house keys are back in the world of light."

"You should look for them, anyway."

"What would be the use of that?"

"Well, I may be wrong about this, mostly because it's been such a long time since I had anyone or anything worth losing, but I seem to remember that looking for the things you'd misplaced was always a frustrating business. For instance, I was forever losing my screwdriver and never having any luck finding it in any of the places where I would normally expect to find it."

"So?"

"After a while, I would always give up on looking for my screwdriver, and look for something else instead. I'd decide I wanted a piece of cake, and open my refrigerator to see if I had any. And there, right up front, would be a nice big delicious frosted cake, and right there, stuck in the frosting, would be the screwdriver I'd been using the day before to cut the cake into slices."

This didn't help. "Why would you use a screwdriver to slice cake?"

"Probably because I'd misplaced the cake knife, which, if I recall correctly, I'd been using the day before that to rake leaves. It doesn't matter. The point is that if you've misplaced something you really care about, and can't find it in any of the obvious places, it sometimes makes sense to look for something else instead, because that'll lead you to all the places you never thought of looking before."

Pearlie said, "I am not going to waste any time looking for my *keys*."

No, she decided, what she needed was to keep track of this impossibly confusing room, and find a way to make herself a map that she could use to figure out all the stairs leading up and stairs leading down, and tell the difference between those she'd already searched and those she had yet to search.

To do that, Pearlie needed a pen, even if the closest thing she had to paper was the palm of her hand. As it happened, she'd actually had a favorite pen, a blue-and-white ballpoint with attached highlighter, in her jeans pocket on the night that Gustav Gloom had asked for the family's help in talking to the shadow criminal known as Hieronymus Spector. And though the need for a writing implement hadn't come up since, she had occasionally reached into her pocket and found it waiting there, a comforting reminder of a world she had begun to fear she would never know again.

Unfortunately, when she reached for that pen now, it was gone, fallen through a hole that had ripped open in the bottom of that pocket.

"Great!" she grumbled. "Now I can't find my pen, *either*."

Her shadow leaned down and retrieved

something from the floor at Pearlie's feet. "Here it is. You must have only dropped it a second ago."

"Thank you," Pearlie said, clicking the pen a couple of times to make sure it still worked.

Not-Roger said, "Um. Pearlie?"

"What are you going to suggest now?" Pearlie said in irritation. "That I look in my *shoe*?"

"No," Not-Roger said, "but right *in front of you* might be nice."

Pearlie rolled her eyes. "At what? There's nobody here but you, me, and my shadow, and if . . ."

Pearlie stopped mid-sentence, remembering that the last time she had seen the shadow version of herself was when Lord Obsidian's minions had hauled away her father. The shadow girl had elected to stay with him rather than with the girl whose shape she wore.

After a moment, Pearlie managed, "You!"

"Of course," said the shadow girl. "Who else would I be?"

"You *left* me."

"Only for as long as it took you to catch up. I figured you'd understand: Somebody needed to stay by your dad all this time. I figured he needed somebody to keep an eye on him more than you did. Was I wrong about that?"

It took Pearlie a second to manage an answer of any kind. "Is he okay?"

Pearlie's shadow gestured at the crazy architecture around them: the irregular directionless stairs that headed up in some places and down in others but never seemed to arrive at any destination. "All these stairs, wherever the eye can see, and not a single safety railing to be found? How do you think he's taking it?"

Pearlie had never in her whole life felt so sorry for her father, a professional safety expert who had compiled entire filing cabinets of terrible things that could happen to people who were careless while climbing up or down stairs. Being trapped in a place like this without benefit of safety railings was exactly the kind of thing that would drive her father especially crazy. "Bring me to him!"

"I can't," her shadow said. "He's standing behind you . . ."

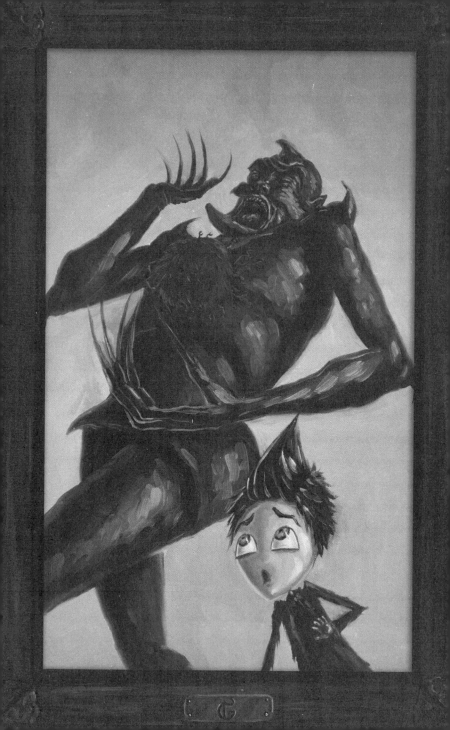

CHAPTER SEVEN
THE SURRENDER OF GUSTAV GLOOM

The Beast was any size it wanted to be and any shape it thought it ought to be. It changed its mind almost constantly, and was with each step not quite the same monster it had been one step earlier, qualities that along with its tremendous speed and power made it an almost impossible creature to either flee or fight.

There was a reason it was the worst monster people could imagine, in any language where people used words to try to describe the monsters glimpsed in dark places, a reason why it had been given so many different names, from bogeyman to Wendigo to Jabberwock: It was everything bad.

But Gustav Gloom had played this game with it before.

Even as it reached for him to cause the pain Lord Obsidian had requested, he had moved out of its way, leaving it to grunt and bellow and galumph about, shattering the statues Lord Obsidian had erected to commemorate the great moments of his life. The baby version of Howard Philip October, the one the aunt had called Little Sunshine, shattered into a thousand pieces. The young scholar his fellow students had avoided exploded into pebbles. The teller of strange tales about alien worlds and ancient civilizations broke in half. Still, the Beast whirled about, with arms that changed shape with every second, trying to get its claws on what it perceived as a bothersome flea that persisted in irritating the top of its head, no matter how desperately the monster struggled to swat it.

Gustav scrambled down the monster's back, evading a grab from an arm that the Beast had grown for the occasion. He couldn't resist taunting Lord Obsidian on the way: "Too bad about your statues, Howie! I could have told you all about your pet's habit of carelessly breaking them! He broke a lot of them back at my house! Maybe I can make him break so many you won't have any left!"

Lord Obsidian didn't stir from his throne. "They will be no trouble to replace."

"But isn't that the point, Howie? They're all

you have! What difference does it make if they get smashed or not? When you were a person, you threw away people . . . and all it earned you in exchange is a bunch of *stupid statues!*"

Frustrated beyond what little reason it had, the Beast turned itself inside out to get to Gustav, an act that left the little halfsie boy inside him. However, the Beast was notoriously stupid, and forgot to close his mouth to trap Gustav inside. Gustav leaped out of the slightly darker spot that represented its mouth, rolled across the floor, and darted between the great monster's legs as it came for him again.

"This is very amusing," Lord Obsidian noted, "but even a boy who is part shadow is still part flesh and blood. You will not be able to keep this up forever."

Gustav didn't point out that he didn't have to, not as long as the Beast had a long history of being as easy to lead as a maddened bull.

Instead, he headed toward the one part of the room that Lord Obsidian would have expected him to avoid: the throne.

Lord Obsidian realized what Gustav was up to in time to clutch for him. Whatever particularly awful kind of shadow he was made of made the air terribly cold around him. His long, spindly, floor-length fingers rotted the material of Gustav's jacket when they brushed his lapels in passing . . . but the same speed that enabled Gustav to play a pretty decent game of keep-away with one monster out of nightmares also permitted him to evade that clutching grasp.

The soles of Gustav's shoes flaked and crumbled as Gustav raced up Lord Obsidian's chest and leaped away from his shoulders. By the time Gustav was airborne, he was barefoot. But that was worth it. The Beast, who had been just a step or two behind him, was as heedless in his pursuit of him as a pet dog is in chasing a pet cat across the bed where its master lies sleeping. The Beast hit the world-conquering former Howard Philip October in the center of his chest. Caught up in the excitement and fury of the chase, it knew only that it had caught *something*, and raked at Lord Obsidian's body with both fangs and claws, as if its master and not Gustav were the prey it had sought.

Lord Obsidian's scream of pain was one of the most terrible sounds Gustav had ever heard. It sounded like gears ripping through steel, like a thousand creatures on fire, like a million stringed instruments all playing the same screeching note at once. It was a sound that must have been heard all over his castle, and likely over much of the Dark Country, as well, and for as long as it went on, Gustav could only hope that his friends and allies were still alive and listening.

Unfortunately, it was over almost immediately, because Obsidian snarled, *"Heel!"* and the Beast immediately obeyed, curling up at his feet like any pet smart enough to understand that it had just been bad.

Gustav hit the ground and rose to his feet in a throne room that was now filled with rubble. "Well, Howie. Are you going to make a dumb statue of *that*?"

Lord Obsidian began to snarl, but then seemed to remember himself, and offered the troublesome boy a naughty wag of his finger instead. "You are a very clever halfsie, Gustav. Well done. But as you will see, it is not even close to enough."

He pressed a button on his armrest, and one of the shadows imprisoned beyond the transparent wall behind the throne was suddenly and violently drawn upward. A second later, it fell from the ceiling above the throne and landed in Lord Obsidian's hand, as convenient as a candy bar dispensed by a vending machine. The shadow trembled and screamed for mercy, but the instant Lord Obsidian pressed it against his injured chest, its substance flowed into his, healing his wound immediately. The face of the victimized shadow was the last part to sink below the surface before it was silenced.

"See?" Lord Obsidian gloated.

Gustav shuddered. "I've got to give you credit. That was pretty disgusting."

"By all human standards, perhaps. But it is part of the reason I've gone to so much effort to conquer this place and imprison so many of the shadows who live here. They are all now just raw materials I can use to replenish myself. Except for a select few, who will follow me into the new universe I intend to build once the old one has been destroyed, they will all soon be part of me. I will add all the other shadows of the Dark Country to what I am, and then I will add all those dwelling in the world of light to what I am, and then I will add the shadow of the entire universe to what I am. In the end, Gustav, there will be nothing left but me, my closest minions, and whatever worlds I decide to create as my temporary playthings."

Gustav blinked. "Sounds lonely. I guess this is the part of the story where I say, 'You're mad.'"

"Why don't you?"

"It's not something I have to say, Howie. I knew you were a crazy old loser before I ever met you."

Lord Obsidian didn't just leap from his throne; he *exploded* from it. He moved faster than the People Taker ever had, faster than the Beast ever had, faster than any shadow Gustav had ever seen. In an instant he had crossed the pitifully short distance separating himself from the boy, and wrapped his impossibly long fingers around Gustav's neck.

Gustav clutched at those awful fingers, trying to peel them from around his neck, but his hands went numb the instant he touched them, and his arms fell to his sides, as useless as rags.

"Do you feel that?" Lord Obsidian snarled. "Do you feel how helpless you are at my touch?"

Gustav tried to answer, but nothing escaped his mouth but a hiss.

"Don't for one second think that your cleverness will make me as easy to evade as my pet. The Beast is just a shadow—a very powerful and dangerous shadow, but still no more than a shadow. I have made myself into something worse than any man or any shadow, something that can take life with a touch. If I wish, contact with my flesh would rot your flesh, as it did your clothing. You would age a lifetime in an instant, and find yourself a withered old man, too weak to stand. Or I could hold on to you even longer and watch as you crumbled to dust."

Gustav's throat had gone dry, as if he now, for the very first time, felt the thirst that had somehow never made itself known at any point since his arrival in the Dark Country. His legs had gone numb, as well. He found that he wasn't afraid of dying, because that had never been something he worried about, but he did feel an awful sadness at the thought of all the people he had failed.

Then Lord Obsidian released him, and he fell to the cold stone floor.

"After all the insults I have suffered from you," Lord Obsidian said, "I am tempted to rescind my generous offer. I don't need a halfsie boy, or even the location of the Nightmare Vault, that much. But I can afford to give you one last chance. You will join me and start following my orders, or I will have the What girls and their father brought here so you can see the worst my touch can do to those who defy me."

Gustav coughed, blinked away the weakness that had overcome him in the few seconds that he'd been imprisoned in Lord Obsidian's grasp, and then managed to pull himself to his feet. He swayed. He was aware that he already looked like he'd been on the losing side of a war. His shoes had almost completely dissolved into dust and were now just a pair of leather rings around his ankles. The lapels of his jacket had faded, and even the rest of his suit looked like it had been nibbled by moths. He raised his arms, just to make sure they still worked, and found that even though the strength and the feeling were returning to them, they were for the moment still moving like the branches of a dead tree stirring from the touch of some cold autumn wind.

It was clear that, up until this moment, Lord Obsidian had just been toying with him.

The conqueror of the Dark Country regarded him closely, just to confirm that all the fight had gone out of him, then offered a satisfied nod and returned to his throne so he could wait for Gustav's answer.

For the first time in a life of perfect health,

Gustav had to speak with a hoarse voice. "Can I . . . tell you a little story first?"

"As long as you tell it to me respectfully."

"When I was very small . . . and just starting to realize that I would never be able to explore the world on the other side of the iron fence . . . my shadow mother used to tell me . . . that nothing's ever really sad."

Lord Obsidian rolled his eyes. "Oh, please."

"She said . . . that even when sad things happen, when life disappoints you or takes away the things you love . . . there's always something happy to look for . . . something you can find and hold on to . . . that can show you your problems aren't nearly as bad as they seem."

"Did any of this insipid foolishness actually help?"

"She said that . . . even if I lost people, then that just meant I had room in my heart for more. She said that . . . even if I was trapped behind a fence . . . it only meant that someday a special person would know where to find me. She said that . . . even if there was evil in the world . . . evil like you . . . then it was only worth noticing because there was also good somewhere, to measure it against."

"I get it," Lord Obsidian said, sounding as tired as any all-powerful conqueror of a shadow dimension ever had. "A silver lining behind every cloud, blah blah blah. This really isn't doing much to improve your situation."

Gustav found himself standing a little straighter, and his voice sounding a little stronger. "I haven't gotten to the point of the story yet."

"If the point is as fascinating as everything I've heard so far, I'm sure I'm in for something special."

Gustav flexed his arms, which had almost completely recovered now, and cleared his throat so his voice could do the same. "For many years, both before and after my shadow mom disappeared, I didn't believe her, not even a little bit. Oh, I was a good kid, and I pretended that what she said made me feel better, but inside I reacted the same way you have. I rolled my eyes. Why wouldn't I? They were just words. They didn't change any of the problems I had to live with. I was still alone. Still trapped behind a fence. Still living in a world where it was easy to see evil and hard to see good."

"We had better be near the end now."

"Many years later," Gustav said, "after my

shadow mother disappeared, I found out she'd been right about every single last bit of it."

He took a deep breath and concluded: "All it took was for Fernie What to move in across the street."

There was a moment of silence. Then Lord Obsidian clapped. "That's it? Am I supposed to weep? See the error of my ways? Apologize for everything I've done, free the Dark Country, and return your loved ones to you?"

"That would be nice," Gustav admitted, "but I don't expect it. No, I just wanted you to know what Fernie and her family showed me: that even if you're right, and I find myself having to surrender to you, my shadow mother still knew what she was talking about. There's a good side to everything, even this."

"And before I reduce you to a pile of ash just for wasting my time with this drivel, what silver lining do you find in the knowledge that you now stand defeated before me?"

Gustav told him, "At least I got to destroy your statues."

And for long minutes, the throne room of Lord Obsidian was rocked by the dark one's mocking laughter.

CHAPTER EIGHT
FERNIE DELIVERS AN IMPORTANT MESSAGE

Hans Gloom didn't seem to be in any hurry to wake up, even with company visiting the shadow version of the house inside the house for what must have been the first time ever.

"He has been asleep a long time," Penny's shadow explained. "I keep him asleep, because it's better for him to sleep and dream of his happy times with the flesh-and-blood Penny, than to wake up and remember everything that's happened to him since."

Fernie regarded the pale, fragile figure. Unlike Not-Roger, who had been in the Dark Country for decades and didn't seem to have aged a year in all that time, Hans Gloom had been imprisoned in a place specifically designed to drain the life and hope from people, and he showed the effects. He had aged since posing for the photographs she had seen of him; not just the ten years that had passed since he chased Howard Philip October to the Dark Country, but more like twenty. His hair had gone silver, and his face had become drawn and lined. But he was still clearly the man who had loved a woman named Penny and fathered a child named Gustav—a man whose strength and goodness were not gone, but simply hidden beneath a curtain of sleep. "I didn't know shadows could cast sleeping spells."

"This is not quite a sleeping spell, Fernie. I could not force any man to sleep if he did not actually prefer to be asleep. But have you never been in bed past the moment when it was time to wake up, unwilling to open your eyes because your dream was too special to surrender without a fight? That is what Hans is doing. He chases the shadows of happiness I have placed in his head, and stays sleeping for as long as he knows that the only thing to greet his waking eyes is heartache and loss. This has been protecting him from the madness of this place for years."

Even in her journeys across the Dark Country, it had been quite some time since Fernie had heard anything quite so terrible. "Could he wake up if he wanted?"

"It is always his choice, Fernie. But the price of this gift I have given him is that he will stay asleep until he has some reason for hope."

Fernie shuddered. "Please don't give me the same gift. As bad as this place is, I'd rather not sleep my whole life away."

"If you are here for any real length of time, you may yet find yourself asking for it. But, no, Fernie; we have too much to talk about for us to take that measure right away."

The two of them left Hans Gloom to his slumber and went outside to where all good conversations take place in that kind of house, the porch swing. Their surroundings didn't seem as peaceful as such a place should. On the porch of a real country house, the air smells fresh and the sky feels open and the air rings with the sounds of the local insects and birds. Even on the porch of the real house inside the house that Fernie remembered from Gustav's home, where the grass was a carpet and the horizon was just a painted backdrop, the house itself had felt like a peaceful and inviting place that had once been warmed by the comforts of family. Here, the air was gray and the sky seemed closed, and the only thing Fernie felt was the oppressive awfulness just outside the illusion Penny's shadow had created. But she was surprised to find that there was love here, too: the fierce love the shadow woman felt for the man she sheltered and the child she had lost.

For several minutes Penny's shadow listened intently as Fernie summarized her adventures with Gustav, from the moment of their first meeting to their encounter with Scrofulous. Then she shook her head. "You should have stayed in your world of light, Fernie. Even before Lord Obsidian arrived in the Dark Country and ravaged the countryside with his mad wars of conquest, this was never a place a fallen human being could ever escape. Shadows can pass back and forth with ease, but from here there's no way for a being of flesh and blood to rise back to the realm of sunlight."

"There's always the Cryptic Carousel," Fernie said, referring to the vehicle she and Gustav had used to get to the Dark Country.

Penny's shadow shook her head. "How dearly I wish I'd known about the things you say the carousel can do. Back when Gustav was small, and I was just a mother trying to take care of her boy, I never imagined it to be more than a playful amusement-park ride, left in some out-of-the-way room for the children of the Gloom family to play with. Had I been aware of its true powers long ago, I would have found a way to pilot it to the Dark Country and give poor Hans a lift back. But where is that wondrous machine now, Fernie? Do you even have the means to signal it and alert the shadow at its controls to where he can find you?"

It seemed like a million years must have passed since Fernie had last seen it lifting into the sky under the expert hand of Grandpa Lemuel's shadow. It was, even now, awaiting a signal from Gustav. But Gustav had never specified what signal because he had not known what he and Fernie would find once they entered the Dark Country. Fernie had no useful ideas. So she shook her head.

"So," Penny's shadow said, "we are left with the same problem. You should have accepted the loss of your father and sister, and returned to living your life for however long both our worlds survive the destruction the fiend plans."

"That's a fine thing for you to say," declared Fernie, who had put together everything she already knew about Gustav's past and was pretty sure she'd figured out what chain of events had led to his shadow mother's imprisonment in this place. "You didn't have to come here, either. You were the only real loving relative Gustav had. Nobody could have ever blamed you for staying with him and out of trouble. But then you found out where Hans was. And you decided you couldn't let another day pass without heading for the Dark Country yourself to rescue him."

Penny's shadow faced the shadow of the fake lawn, beneath the fake walls bearing the fake farmland, beneath the fake light of the room's shadow sun. Her profile was delicate and as lovely as the profile of the flesh-and-blood woman must have been, but there was an awful fragility to her, the sense that she could have been blown away by the first angry wind. "Love is like a chain binding you to others. If someone you care about falls into a terrible place, it can pull you in after them."

This Fernie understood to be true, because it had been the plight of her family that had led her to enter the Dark Country herself. "How did it happen to you?"

"There were always rumors, my dear girl:

tales of two men from the world of light who had brought their personal war to the most desolate parts of the Dark Country. I knew they had to be Hans and Howard Philip October. But for many years, Gustav was too small a child for me to abandon, even on such an errand of mercy."

Fernie said, "You wanted to, though."

"Of course I wanted to," Penny's shadow said. "Penny loved Hans Gloom with all her heart, and while I was with her I saw enough of the man he was to love him just as deeply. But it was always my duty to take care of his son. So for years I did what I supposed he would have wanted, and remained with Gustav.

"But then the nature of the stories coming out of the Dark Country changed. The tales of the good man chasing the bad one became instead tales of the evil man transforming into something far worse than either human or shadow; tales of him beginning his wars of conquest; tales of the good man raising an army of shadows himself, to face the evil one's forces in a series of battles that left large parts of the Dark Country in ruins.

"Hans had become a legendary hero of the Dark Country by then, one whose courage was admired even by shadows who dwelt in the world of light . . . but even so, I stayed away, because in some of those stories the good man already seemed to have a chance of winning. I stayed with Gustav and told myself that Hans didn't need my help."

Shadows didn't breathe, but Penny's shadow heaved a deep sigh anyway, before continuing.

"Then, one day, when Gustav was only five, I found out that Lord Obsidian had captured Hans in a terrible ambush and was about to sentence him to this chamber around us, where men are driven insane by the sounds of hopelessness.

"Only I could save my beloved's mind, by rushing to his side and joining him in his prison, where I could create this illusion to protect him. But to get here in time to make a difference, I had to leave right away. Gustav was off playing in the mansion's yard, so there was no time to tell him where I was going. I could only stop to tell dear Great-Aunt Mellifluous to take care of him . . . and to keep him safe from the knowledge of where his flesh father and shadow mother had gone.

"I have ached for word of my son ever since, Fernie . . . and until your arrival have had none in all the years I have been here protecting the man who fathered him."

She fell silent, but it was clear that she still had one last thing, perhaps the worst thing, left to say.

Fernie had learned in her travels with Gustav that even shadows were capable of great fear, and Gustav's shadow mother wore the awful look of a person who needed to struggle to face hers.

Fernie waited for as long as it took.

After a long time, Penny's shadow asked, "Tell me, sweet girl, does he hate me?"

Fernie pulled back in astonishment. "What? Who? You mean Gustav?"

"Of course. Does he hate me?"

"That's the craziest thing I ever— Why would he hate you?"

"For leaving him. For not telling him where I had gone. For never saying good-bye."

Fernie took both of the shadow woman's hands and held them tightly. She felt the warmth and the solidity of them even though they were not flesh, and understood for the first time what it had been like for young Gustav to have her as a mother. Fernie found herself missing her own mother, and her father, so much that hot tears spilled from her eyes, and she was barely able to find the voice she needed. "He doesn't hate you. I promise. He misses you. He never blamed you for anything."

"Really?"

"Really. Until I finally told him to quit it, he never blamed anybody but himself."

The shadow woman's eyes widened and for a moment grew shiny with grief and shame and pity. "Oh, that poor lovely boy!"

She might have gone on, but a terrible cry of pain sounded from somewhere beyond the illusion of the house inside the house, chilling Fernie's blood. It was the rage and indignation of an evil being who had never imagined that any enemy could be capable of hurting him, and though it was one of the worst sounds Fernie had ever heard, it was also somehow one of the best, because it was capable of returning the hope to her heart.

Penny's shadow was startled into losing concentration: The shadow illusion of the painted room and the porch of the house inside the house wavered, and the awful presences that actually filled this place briefly became visible, their faces drawn and dark and mad.

After what felt like about half a minute, Penny's shadow managed to regain control of the illusion, and the porch returned, though it now seemed thinner and weaker and shakier than before.

"What was that?" she whispered.

Fernie realized that her cheeks hurt from grinning so hard. "*That* was the best thing that ever could have happened."

"What? How could that possibly be—"

The screen door of the country house swung open, and Hans Gloom stepped out.

He looked groggy and wan and confused, and when he saw Penny's shadow standing with both her fists against her mouth, he brightened for a second or two before seeming to remember that she was just a shadow and that the real woman he'd loved was dead.

His eyes flickered toward Fernie, and though he could not possibly have recognized her, his eyes warmed when he saw that she was flesh and blood. It took him a couple of tries to find his voice. "I'm sorry . . . but I recognized that sound. It's grown more terrible . . . but I heard a version of it often enough. That was . . . *October* screaming. Like something had just hurt him. How . . ."

Fernie didn't waste a moment. She marched right up to him and stuck out her hand. Hans stared as if not quite certain what he was supposed to do, then seemed to remember the proper response and returned the handshake with the awe and wonder that could only come to a man who had almost forgotten the sensation of being touched by another human being.

Fernie said, "Hello."

Hans's voice trembled. "Pleased . . . to meet you, miss. What's your name?"

Fernie beamed. "You're right. What *is* my name."

"What?"

"Exactly. *Fernie* What."

"Excuse me. Your name is *What*?"

Her cheeks ached from the width of her smile. "You grew up living in a house where the shadows walk and talk, and that's the part you have trouble believing?"

Hans Gloom blinked a number of times, unnerved to see such happiness in such an unpleasant place. "And . . . ummm . . . who are you, again?"

"I'm best friends with your son, Gustav."

He stumbled over the name. "G-Gustav?"

"Uh-huh. He turned out to be one of the coolest kids *ever*, and he brought me here to find you and bring you back home."

"What?"

"That's still my name. And you heard me right the first time. Your son sent me."

Shock robbed the strength from his legs. He fell back against the doorframe, which gave off little puffs of gray as the impact disturbed it. "N-no. It can't be. This is just another of October's tricks. My unborn son died with Penny." A glance at the shadow version of his beloved wife, who continued to regard him with undisguised love, and he hastily corrected himself: "I'm sorry. I don't m-mean you. I mean the flesh-and-blood Penny, of course. The baby died when she did."

"No, he didn't," Fernie said. "He's alive and he's terrific and he kicks butt, and you know what else? That scream we just heard?"

"Yes?"

"That's the sound Lord Obsidian makes when *your son* catches up with him and takes up the job you started."

Hans Gloom whipped his gaze toward Penny's shadow, seeking confirmation of the truth he didn't dare to believe . . . and after a moment the shadow woman closed her eyes and nodded.

He slid down the doorframe, landing on his knees. "I have a son?"

"Yes." Fernie grinned. "You have a son, and he's more amazing than you could possibly imagine."

"Believe her," Penny's shadow said. "It's true."

Hans Gloom resisted it for another heartbeat or two, shaking his head as if the news were terrible instead of a reason for hope. He whispered, "I have a son." Then testing the phrase out, as if the shape of the words felt unfamiliar in his mouth, he said it louder. "I have a son." The world didn't end just because he said it, and so he stood up, sweeping Fernie off her feet and lifting her into the air with arms that had suddenly regained their strength. *"I have a son!"*

Fernie didn't mind the hug. Hugs were in terribly short supply in this place. What mattered more was something Fernie knew at once, from the tears brimming in the man's eyes and the joy lighting up a face that had known no joy for far too long: that he was every bit as good a man as he had been advertised to be, and would, if given a chance, be a great dad.

She dearly wished she had more time to let him enjoy the news. But she didn't, so she hit him with the even more important part: "So you have a son. But now that you know about him, are you going to go back to sleep and allow him to face Lord Obsidian alone, or are we going to break out of here and do something to help him?"

CHAPTER NINE
MORE HORRIBLE THAN ANY MAN COULD EVER POSSIBLY IMAGINE

Hans Gloom's smile froze on his face, replaced by a determined grimace. He put Fernie down and turned to Penny's shadow. "Can we?"

The shadow woman shook her head and backed away a step, as if the mere suggestion was so horrible that the issue could never be considered. "Please don't ask me that, Hans."

"If the answer was no, you would have said so already. There's something else going on, something you haven't told us yet. Tell me."

She fell onto the porch swing and shuddered. "You must understand. I was . . . never actually captured by Lord Obsidian. I came here willingly and snuck into this chamber without him knowing. I was here at the moment you were thrown in, and I made sure that you never experienced a moment of this chamber's torments. He never bothered to check on you, and therefore he never knew that I was here giving you some measure of peace. He never chained me like the ones whose screams were supposed to drive you mad. I was always able to leave."

Hans Gloom nodded with each new sentence. "You're Penny's shadow, all right. You're as brave and as selfless as she was, and I'll always love you for it. But if you could always leave, why didn't you ever go just long enough to find some way to free me?"

Penny's shadow wouldn't look at him. She looked as defeated, as miserable, as Fernie had seen her. "Because I've always been the only thing that protected you here. If I leave even for a minute or less, all this"—she gestured with her arms, indicating the shadow version of the house inside the house—"goes away, and you'll be alone against the full effects of this room. I can't do that. It could destroy you in no time at all. Especially now that I also have the sanity of an innocent girl to think of . . ."

Fernie understood what had kept Penny's shadow trapped inside this room for so long: the chains of love she had spoken of. "He won't be alone if the innocent girl is with him."

Penny's shadow glanced from man to girl and back to man, desperate to find the words that would allow them to understand. She looked at her hands. "But . . . you don't know, either of you . . . it'll be worse than any man could ever imagine!"

Hans Gloom knelt beside the shadow woman and lifted her chin with his finger, to make her gaze meet his. "And if you actually believe I wouldn't willingly go through worse than any man could ever imagine, just to lay eyes on my son and be a true father to him, then maybe you don't know me very well at all."

"Or me," Fernie declared. "I have a *sister* out there somewhere, and I'm *bored* with this place."

Penny's shadow turned away from Hans and studied Fernie closely, as if looking for some sign of uncertainty or madness. Whatever she happened to be looking for, she didn't seem to find, because a look of reluctant wonder spread across her lovely features, and she murmured, "So this is the kind of friend my boy Gustav makes for himself. I'm beginning to think . . . that Lord Obsidian's in big trouble."

Over the next few minutes, Fernie What and Hans Gloom knelt on the shadow version of the fake lawn that surrounded the house inside the house, and prepared for what both understood to be the greatest challenge of their lives. They held on tightly, knowing that in the next few seconds, staying close to each other might be the only thing capable of protecting their respective minds. Mr. Gloom looped his arms under Fernie's and reached up with his forearms to hold both hands over her ears; Fernie returned the favor by plugging both of his with her index fingers.

Just to see how soundproof this arrangement was, Fernie chanted a phrase that had always come in handy whenever Pearlie was particularly annoying. "La-la-la-la-la, I can't *hear* you."

Hans Gloom took his hands off her ears. "You just said *la-la-la-la-la, I can't hear you.*"

Fernie removed her fingers from his ears. "I don't suppose you have any cotton balls or earplugs or anything."

"Sorry. I didn't get a chance to pack before I fell into the Dark Country. You're not changing your mind about trying to escape, are you?"

"Nope."

"Okay," he said. "So let's try this, then. Instead of trying to drown out the screams by saying something meaningless, chant the name of something meaningful. Chant the name of somebody who's depending on you. Think of nothing but that name, and concentrate on saying it, over and over again, as loudly as you can. If the screams get through anyway, you can tell yourself that they're just a bunch of crazy shadows and that you've already faced monsters worse than the likes of them."

Fernie also had advice to offer. "Also, it's okay to scream really loud. I ride roller coasters all the time, and I've found out it's less scary if you scream and make screaming a fun thing to do."

"I'll keep that in mind," he said gravely. "Good luck, Fernie What."

"Good luck, Hans Gloom."

The front yard of the shadow version of the house inside the house—which was not just a fake lawn like the original, but a fake of the *fake*— seemed to contract to about half its prior size, as Penny's shadow gathered up her substance for a leap at the exit. The awful sounds she had blocked out grew a little easier to hear, enough to chill Fernie when she considered just how bad they would sound when they were no longer blocked at all. Penny's shadow drew close and brushed a transparent hand against Mr. Gloom's shoulder and Fernie's curly hair. The shadow woman knit her brow in concern and said, "I should be able to return in two minutes or less, but there's no telling what's waiting for me on the other side of the hatch. If I'm stopped, or if I can't come back at all . . ."

Hans Gloom finished the sentence for her: ". . . you would have already done more than I ever could have asked of you."

Penny's shadow turned to Fernie next. "And you, Fernie? Are you ready?"

She gulped. "Why not?"

Penny's shadow waited until Hans Gloom had once again covered Fernie's ears with his hands, and Fernie had once again plugged his ears with her fingers. Then, on the count of three, she left. The shadow version of the house inside the house and the room that surrounded it went liquid and flowed toward the shadow woman like dirty water circling a drain, then started to spill upward as she slipped through the crack in the hatch.

Then it was gone, and she was gone, and all that remained was the Screaming Room.

Fernie had already experienced a few seconds of it once, but Penny's shadow must have rescued her before it got too bad, because the difference between that experience and this one was like the difference between getting a few freckles from the sun and being burned lobster red. The sounds made by the shadows imprisoned in this room were the screams of things that had never known a single moment of hope or joy, things that knew that every moment they endured imprisonment was going to be worse than all the moments that had ever come before.

In no time at all, Fernie started screaming, too, and not because it put her in control of her fear, the way she was on roller coasters. She screamed because the sounds they made really were worse than anything she had ever known.

She felt her mind start to go, and vaguely remembered a bit of advice she'd been given about chanting the name of somebody who was depending on her. But though the faces came to her, the names did not. She remembered a kind and protective man who seemed to do nothing but worry about her but whose presence had always made her feel safe and loved. She remembered a brave and adventurous woman who had always told her that she could be anything she wanted to be. She remembered a girl very much like herself, only taller, who was smart and funny and an example of everything she wanted to become. But the names of her father and mother and sister receded from her, knocked right out of her head by the terrible sounds she could not cast out. The only name available to her was one that she might not have been able to remember on her own, but that the man before her kept shouting in a voice like thunder.

"GUSTAV! GUSTAV! GUSTAV!"

She found her voice. *"GUSTAV! GUSTAV! GUSTAV!"*

They each chanted the name separately, and then somehow found a rhythm and started chanting it together. *"GUSTAV! GUSTAV! GUSTAV!"*

His voice and her voice became one big voice, standing alone against everything that was destructive and terrible.

Then she was ripped from the small comfort of the chant into what felt like the worst nightmare of all time, in which she was chased through a dark place filled with jagged shapes and horrible faces by a monster who would not stop chasing her no matter how fast she ran. She didn't know what the thing was, only that it was much larger than herself and intent on devouring her. She lashed out at it, heard it roar in response, and

shrieked as its clawed hands reached for her:
"GUSTAV! GUSTAV! GUSTAV!"

A familiar voice cried: *"Fernie!* That's enough!"

She had the sense that whoever it was had been trying to make herself heard over her own nonstop shouting of Gustav's name.

She blinked the mental cobwebs away and realized that she was now lying flat on her back in some dim alcove, not far from the hatch. Two figures knelt beside her, one on each side. Hans Gloom, who looked even paler than he had before, knelt to her left, patting her hand, and Penny's shadow knelt on her right, brushing her cheek with a touch like a soft summer breeze.

She wouldn't exactly call the alcove quiet. She could still hear the creaks and echoes of the castle, as well as the cries of distant prisoners. But after the Screaming Room, the relative silence felt wonderful. She realized that she'd failed to notice it for several minutes now, as Hans Gloom and Penny's shadow labored in vain to make her realize that the worst was over.

The shadow woman drew closer. "Fernie? Do you know where you are?"

"I'm . . . somewhere in Lord Obsidian's castle, I guess. Deep in the Dark Country, but it looks like we've gotten out of the Screaming Room. Am I right?"

Penny's shadow looked like she was about to cry. "Yes, honey. Yes. You're right. That's where we are, just down the hall from the Screaming Room. I'm so happy you came back to us. For a while there we both thought we'd lost you."

Fernie winced in genuine pain. "Ow."

"What's wrong?"

"I bit my cheek. I have one of those lumps on it now, that I'll have to keep on accidentally biting all day. I *hate* when that happens."

Hans Gloom flashed a smile, which was by far one of the brightest things Fernie had ever seen in the Dark Country. There was a fresh set of parallel scratches on his left cheek, running almost all the way from his ear to the corner of his lips. "Me too, honey. How are you doing, aside from that?"

"I've also got a sore throat from yelling. Wait. We were yelling *a lot*. Shouldn't we be worried about the guards coming to investigate?"

"We would," Penny's shadow said, "if you'd been doing any of that yelling anywhere but just outside the Screaming Room, or down this corridor where all the most despised prisoners are kept. I'm afraid that screaming and yelling is an expected part of the local atmosphere down here. It wouldn't worry anybody unless those sounds suddenly stopped."

Now that Penny's shadow mentioned it, Fernie could hear distant muffled cries coming from every direction; her own yelling, loud as it was, wouldn't have added much.

She shuddered at the thought of a place so terrible that it was more disturbing for screams to stop than for them to start. "What about all the shadows still chained in the Screaming Room? Shouldn't we try to rescue them, too?"

"They're so mad, they would fight us if we tried. Freeing them, and curing them of their insanity, is something that's going to have to wait for another time. Meanwhile, you need to concentrate on getting back your strength so we can move on and not waste this escape on gestures that would just leave the two of you trapped again."

Fernie hated to leave any creature, even a mad shadow, behind in the Screaming Room, but had to admit to herself that Penny's shadow was right.

A few seconds later she noticed something

else that could be important, something that had been next to invisible inside the illusion Penny's shadow made. She asked Hans, "Where's your shadow, anyway?"

"I don't know," said Hans Gloom. "Where's yours?"

"In the world of light, somewhere. She was missing for a while even before I left to come here. Where did you last see yours?"

"Just before Lord Obsidian's forces captured me. I saw that I was about to be taken, and told my shadow to flee and save himself. He said that he would continue the fight as best he could, but that's the last I heard. I don't know what's happened to him."

"I hope he's okay," said Fernie.

"So do I," said Hans Gloom. "But I guess that's one of the many things I'll have to wait to find out."

Fernie glanced at Penny's shadow, noting for the first time just how much the shadow of Gustav's mother bore on her face the features echoed on Gustav's. Even so, the sight of a shadow, any shadow, brought back some of the horror Fernie had experienced in the Screaming Room. "How long were we in there without your protection?"

Penny's shadow said, "A little less than two minutes, dear girl."

"It . . . felt like a *lot* more than that."

"I was back almost immediately. But by the time I returned to the room and opened the hatch for you, you were so out of your mind with terror that you didn't recognize Hans anymore. The poor man had to chase you into the worst part of the room's madness just to rescue you."

Fernie turned back to Hans Gloom and considered the kind of courage it would take any man to run headlong into madness just to save a little girl he barely knew. She supposed it would have required even more bravery, even more disregard of his own safety, than running into a burning building to save somebody, because a hero who failed to make his way back out of a burning building could only give up his life, but somebody who failed to make his way out of the Screaming Room would be stuck in there forever.

She gave a second hard look at the scratches on Hans Gloom's cheek, and winced. "Don't tell me I gave you those."

"Don't worry," said Hans Gloom, with a wink. "It wasn't something I ever planned to tell you."

Some occasions require a teary hug before

anybody involved can move on to anything else. This was one of them. It wasn't the first teary hug Fernie had given or received in the Dark Country, or even the first hug she had given Hans Gloom. But like all teary hugs, it made things a little bit better for as long as it lasted. Fernie had to remind herself that this was exactly the kind of thing Lord Obsidian didn't seem to want in the world, any world, anymore, and the thought was so sad that for a moment she hugged Hans Gloom even more tightly before letting go to wipe her eyes dry.

"Okay," she said, as he helped her to her feet. "On to the next thing."

"I agree," he said, giving a few light brushes to her shoulders to clean off some of the dust. "Have any ideas?"

Fernie said, "Don't you want to help Gustav?"

"I'm *desperate* to help Gustav, Fernie. I'm desperate just to *meet* him for the first time. But I also know the difference between doing something that'll get us captured right away and doing something useful. The problem is, I'm out of practice when it comes to whatever one's supposed to do in enemy castles where evil minions hold a thousand-to-one advantage.

Right now, I don't even have the *beginnings* of a plan. Do you?"

Fernie felt a grin spread across her face as she remembered Gustav's odd explanations of the difference between an *idea* and a *plan*.

She said, "Yes."

It happened to be a brilliant plan, too: starting with the release of the screaming shadows as a distraction, moving on past freeing Pearlie and, with any luck, Dad, and finally leading an entire army of the chained and oppressed to a final confrontation with Lord Obsidian.

It was a perfectly brilliant plan in that it was also the *way she wanted things to work out*, and how they really would have worked out had life been more like books.

But unfortunately, it wasn't going to be that simple.

Because even as she took a deep breath and started to launch into it, a squad of Lord Obsidian's minions drifted around the nearest bend of the corridor.

"Well, now," said Gnulbotz, as the minions behind him unsheathed their swords. "This is convenient. We were just coming to fetch you . . ."

CHAPTER TEN
REUNION

Over at the Dungeon of Those Who Await, a familiar and beloved voice said, "Pearlie?"

She still didn't trust what she was hearing until Not-Roger gently stepped forward and turned her around, forcing her to face the man who stood before her with a disbelieving expression that mirrored her own.

He had been through a rough time since they'd been apart, that was certain. Scraped knees showed through rips in his trousers, and the left lens of his eyeglasses had popped out of its frame at some point, which looked particularly odd since the existing right lens worked like a magnifying glass, and the absence of the left one made him look like he had eyes of two completely different sizes. He also wore only one shoe, and his own shadow, clinging close to him like a protective babysitter, looked as frayed at the edges as an old sleeve. But aside from all that he was the man she knew. "Pearlie."

She whispered, *"Daddy."*

Both What girls usually called their father "Dad" these days; they hadn't used the more childlike "Daddy" since kindergarten. But Pearlie was perfectly happy to feel like a much littler girl right now, as she and her father staggered toward each other and did what came naturally.

They were only vaguely aware of Caliban and Anemone and Not-Roger and his shadow, all arriving together just about then, applauding.

The next few minutes went pretty much the way they had to.

First, father and daughter hugged, and they were splendid hugs indeed, salted with tears and many cries of "Are you all right?" that were inevitably answered by "I'm fine, fine, what about you?"

This was a moment of perfect happiness.

Alas, the time then came for each of them to have a few seconds being less than perfectly happy, which Mr. What took care of by saying how sorry he was that Pearlie had gotten caught, and Pearlie took care of by telling her father how sorry she was that it had taken her so long to find him.

This was followed by the time it took for each of them to spend a few minutes describing just what they'd been up to since they'd been separated, which in Mr. What's case wasn't all that long as he'd been trapped in a dungeon with Pearlie's shadow and nothing useful to do but keep hoping for the best, and in Pearlie's case required an explanation of the word *gnarfle*.

Hearing the explanation of the monstrous gnarfle, Mr. What said, "That doesn't sound like it was much fun to deal with at all."

"It wasn't that bad," said Pearlie.

"I miss the poor beast," said Not-Roger. "One of the best pets I ever had."

Then came the part of the conversation where Pearlie had to introduce the patiently waiting Not-Roger to her father, and Not-Roger had to explain that, yes, Not-Roger was really the closest thing to a name he still seemed to have.

They all heard a horrible distant scream, just around then, and realized that something significant had happened, probably involving Gustav . . . but there was nothing that could be done about that right away, so they arrived at the next part of the conversation, the one that wasn't about the father and daughter catching up.

First the human beings and their shadow allies found a part of the dungeon that could accommodate them all in privacy. It was an alcove under a stairway that didn't head up or down or sideways but simply twisted, as if it had had a terrible argument with itself and lost. All around them, lost shadows and the occasional trapped human being traveled the aimless steps that headed from no place special to nowhere in particular, moaning about the heartbreak of knowing that there was no way out.

Anemone explained that Scrofulous had condemned her and Caliban and Not-Roger's shadow to the Dungeon of Those Who Await only a few minutes after condemning Pearlie and Not-Roger there. "Of course," she said, "I knew you and Not-Roger were somewhere around here, so we've been looking for you. We followed the commotion we heard. We spotted your dad from a distance and were hurrying to catch up with him, just before he found you."

"That was convenient," opined Not-Roger.

Anemone patted him on the wrist. "Not all that convenient, dear. It still leaves us in the dungeon of one of the most evil beings who ever existed."

"It does save us a little bother," said Not-Roger. "But isn't that the way it always works? Whenever two groups of people are trying to find each other in a crowded place, it's always best if one stays put. That way they're not *both* looking and unknowingly chasing each other in circles, looking in all the places that they can't possibly know the other bunch has just *left*. The group helping Pearlie and the group helping Pearlie's dad could have looked for each other *forever*, that way."

"What's most convenient," Pearlie said, "is that Anemone here managed to recognize my father without ever meeting him before."

"I *have* met him before," Anemone said.

"Really?" Mr. What said. "I don't remember you."

"You wouldn't," Pearlie said. "At least, you wouldn't remember her wearing this face or calling herself by this name. But just before we all got ourselves captured, I heard Fernie *figuring out* who she really is—a shadow we all know well, who's only *disguising* herself as this stranger Anemone."

Mr. What went through the process of elimination in his head, and exclaimed, "You don't mean Great-Aunt Melli—"

"You're right," Anemone said quickly, her lovely features blurring to provide them all with a quick glimpse of the sweet old-woman shadow who had watched over Gustav in his mother's absence. "But don't say it out loud. I'm one of the leaders of the anti-Obsidian resistance. If his minions ever found out who I truly was, they would lock me, and you, in a much more terrible place than this."

Aware that there might be any number of spies planted among the thousands of other shadows trapped in this dungeon, Pearlie lowered her voice. "Then what were you *doing* among the refugees fleeing the Dark Country? Why did you go with us when Gustav asked that mob for help?"

Anemone lowered her voice, too, and leaned closer to Pearlie and Mr. What. "Two reasons, dear. First, your unfortunate arrival in the Dark Country interrupted another very important mission of mine, one so vital it could change the entire course of the war: helping my friend Caliban here sneak past enemy lines and into Lord Obsidian's castle, to complete an urgent mission of his own."

Pearlie's shadow gave the mysterious Caliban, whose face was still lost in the blackness under his hood, an impressed look. "You must be pretty important."

He shook his head. "No, I'm not. It's defeating Obsidian that's important."

Anemone patted his wrist. "You *are* important, dear. If the fight against Lord Obsidian means anything, it's that *everybody's* important, and not just the beings who seize power and declare their wants and needs more important than anybody else's.

"In any event," she continued, "getting Caliban into the castle was considered so crucial that when Cousin Cyrus contacted me to say that the two of you had fallen into the Pit and were on your way to the Dark Country, I couldn't spare the time to go and rescue you myself; I had to invoke one of Cyrus's many debts to me and pledge *him* to rush to your side instead."

"He was unpleasant about it," Pearlie

admitted, "but he did do everything he could to help."

"Cousin Cyrus is always unpleasant about paying his debts," Anemone said, "but he can be trusted to pay them, as you would know very well if you ever worked out a way for him to owe you something."

Pearlie, who had indeed worked out a way for Cousin Cyrus to owe her something, and had made brilliant use of that debt, said only, "I know."

"A while later I got another message from the world of light, this one sent by the house's terrible butler, Hives. According to him, Gustav and Fernie had found the Cryptic Carousel and had embarked on a journey to rescue you two. I wasn't happy to hear that. I would have preferred for Gustav and Fernie to stay out of danger. But as long as they were on their way, I *hoped* to reunite them with you, Pearlie, and send all of you back home on the carousel, after a stern talking-to."

Pearlie said, "But Dad had been captured by then. Sending us away would have meant making us run away before we could even try to rescue him."

"That," Mr. What said, "would have been perfectly all right with me."

"But not with me," Pearlie said. "And not with Fernie and not with Gustav, who had his own dad to think of."

"I've never met Gustav's dad," Mr. What told her, sadly, "but I think I can speak for him and for all dads when I assure you he would have been okay with all of you running away, too. That's the way being a dad works, honey."

There was a moment of silence as Pearlie considered arguing with this, felt just as strongly that it had been right to attempt a rescue, and understood that what her father had said was correct, too. It wasn't an argument worth having. She looked at Anemone and said, "But you didn't catch up with us in time, did you?"

"No," Anemone said. "Caliban and I ran into some trouble on our way out of the Dark Country, and didn't catch up with any of you until Gustav had already sent the Cryptic Carousel away. After that, the only hope of saving any of you from a lifetime of imprisonment in this lightless world was to follow you . . . and do what we could to make sure that you got to meet up with the carousel again. That included making sure that

Cousin Cyrus didn't quit on you in all that time. When we were together, on our way to Shadow's Inn, he *always* knew who I really was, and that I was watching him for any sign of betrayal."

"You still pretended you didn't know us," Pearlie said accusingly. "You still pretended you weren't interested in helping us."

Anemone nodded. "That's because, as much as I couldn't help worrying about you, I still had my other mission to think of. I still had Caliban with me, and still had to get him into Lord Obsidian's castle undetected. I didn't *dare* confide in you, because the shadow who then called himself Olaf was with us, and I didn't trust him at all. I didn't know he was Nebuchadnezzar, but I still suspected he was up to no good. It wouldn't have been smart to let somebody I suspected of being a spy know who I really was and why I was there."

There was nothing Pearlie could say to that.

Anemone continued. "The mission was why we also had those three nameless shadows with us. You've probably forgotten them by now, as they didn't do or say much while we were all together on that long walk to Shadow's Inn. But they were my messengers, with orders to run back and alert the resistance if we ever ran into trouble, got ourselves captured, or for that matter, succeeded in our mission.

"I had to order two of them back to headquarters when you found yourselves facing a hungry gnarfle, because Caliban and I couldn't stay out of that fight; we were duty-bound to help you. But the third one would have stayed behind and watched from a distance to confirm that the raiders from the zippalin took us. No doubt he brought back word of that, as well.

"Now," she concluded at last, "everybody on our side of the war knows that we've made it to Lord Obsidian's castle. They'll all be awaiting word that Caliban's completed his mission. But when they do, they'll launch a full-scale attack."

Not-Roger's shadow whistled. "That must be some mission."

"Of a sort," said Anemone. "You must realize that this is a war like any other. Even if this is one of those exceptionally rare uncomplicated wars where there's a side that's pretty much good and another that's pretty much bad, people everywhere tend to fight harder when there's something to believe in, some flag they can rally behind. In this case, most of the shadows of the

Dark Country have spent so much time being beaten into thinking that Lord Obsidian is this great big unbeatable monster who nobody could ever possibly oppose and survive, that they've lost hope. They need reminding of the one man who Lord Obsidian ever regarded with fear."

Pearlie, Pearlie's shadow, Not-Roger, and Not-Roger's shadow all spoke the name in unison. *"Hans Gloom."*

They were all looking at one another in wonder and amazement when Mr. What, who'd been listening to Anemone's story with the air of a man who wasn't successfully following much of it, said, "You mean, Gustav's father?"

"The very man," Caliban confirmed.

"But if he's been a prisoner for so many years . . . then he's *already* been defeated. Even if he's alive, he's got to be a wreck by now! There's no guarantee that he's still the man he was!"

"He is," Caliban said. "I *know*."

The hooded shadow put so much weight on the word, so much faith, that there was clearly no point in further arguing. Clearly, the plan, vague as it was, would either be enough, or not. Either way, Pearlie realized, it had to be tried. The alternative was just continuing to sit around and wait, hoping for a rescue that might never come.

It was Mr. What who stood first. "Okay, then. If that's the way it has to be, then point me at the person I have to fight and tell me how I have to fight him."

Pearlie could hardly believe she'd heard that from the man so obsessed with safety that he'd once advocated Bubble-Wrap wallpaper to prevent people from accidentally hurting themselves in small rooms, but there he was, making fists, looking fierce, and demanding an enemy to face.

She got up and stood beside him. "Yeah," she said, and taking a deep breath, spoke the words that she suddenly knew would from now on be remembered as the family battle cry: "We'll show 'em what's What."

Gulping, Not-Roger rose to his feet, as well, and nervously took his own position beside the father and daughter, wearing the expression of a man who had done without a cause to fight for longer than most people even get to live. His size and heft should have made him more fearsome than any of the other flesh-and-blood folk around him, but they really didn't. He looked like a fellow who had joined the army because the army had formed around him and the only alternative was allowing it to leave him behind. But he did his best, looking a little reassured when his shadow rushed to his side and grew large to make him look extra fierce.

As Pearlie's shadow and Mr. What's shadow also joined their respective people, Anemone and Caliban rose to face them, and the beautiful young shadow woman offered the most dazzling smile that Pearlie had ever seen on her. It was a smile very much like the indulgent one Pearlie remembered seeing on the face of the shadow Anemone really was, the much older-looking woman Pearlie knew as Great-Aunt Mellifluous . . . and it was just as warm, just as comforting.

Anemone reached beneath the folds of her gown and brought out a glowing object, so beautiful in its welcome familiarity that Pearlie almost cried out in joy.

It was a key.

Anemone even said, "There's a secret passage out of this dungeon . . ."

It would have been absolutely terrific had

she been given the chance to finish what she was saying.

But Anemone didn't get to describe what no doubt would have been a brilliant plan.

She didn't even get to speak another word before the ceiling opened up directly over their heads and the shadow guard known as Krawg, leading a platoon of Lord Obsidian's minions, announced, "Well, it certainly is helpful to see you all in the same place. It saves us the trouble of collecting you individually . . ."

CHAPTER ELEVEN
FERNIE LOSES HER MIND

Between them, the What girls had been taken prisoner an awful lot this summer vacation.

Fernie didn't know exactly how her sister felt about it, but speaking just for herself, it was getting old.

The guards had leashed Fernie and Mr. Gloom, and stuffed Penny's shadow into a glass jar, but these precautions were unimportant. The fact was, there were more than twenty guards, and the chances of pulling off a successful escape from them was just about zero, so all she could do was march along looking angry. This she did very well. If irate facial expressions could be bottled as ultimate weapons, the one she wore—as Gnulbotz and his platoon escorted her, Penny's shadow, and Hans Gloom through the halls of Obsidian's castle—would have laid waste to entire countries.

The corridors they marched through now were narrow, reeking places, more like sewers than dungeons, though there were cells even here. Forlorn faces, some human, some shadow, and some far stranger things, peered through the barred windows of the iron doors, looking like they now had no purpose in their lives other than standing at those windows and looking like they had no other purpose in their lives. Things that looked like torches burned in the narrow section of wall between each set of doors—but what they burned with was not fire, only a form of darkness a little less impenetrable than the darkness all around them.

Fernie managed to glance back at Hans Gloom and noted that he wore no facial expression at all; he just stumbled along with his mouth hanging open, a thin layer of drool escaping from his slack lips. She didn't understand why he was doing that until Gnulbotz chuckled, and said, "See, girl? I told you, earlier today. Nobody can spend any amount of time in the Screaming Room without losing his mind. This poor rotter's head doesn't even have a pair of marbles to rattle together. He's nothing but an empty sack now, and that's the truth. What do you think of that?"

Fernie understood then that Hans was wearing the expression the guards expected of a man who had been confined to the Screaming Room for so long, because he wanted to hide just how much he really was his old self. It struck her as something she should try herself. So she retorted, "You think you're so smart? Well, *elephants*."

Gnulbotz's eyebrows knit together. "Excuse me?"

"You can imprison my body, but you'll never *coffee pot geranium*."

Gnulbotz grimaced, leaving one of the little maggots who lived in his teeth protruding between his upper and lower lips. "I'm afraid I don't understand what you're getting at, little lady."

Fernie thrust out her lower jaw and declared, "As long as there's even one person willing to stand up and fight for our freedom, you'll never *platypus toilet bowl reverberating golf ball*. Never ever EVER, you *vibrating nose faucet*."

Gnulbotz looked as if he was about to protest that Fernie still wasn't making any sense, when an explanation occurred to him and he glanced at Mr. Gloom with something approaching awe. "Less than an *hour*," he marveled. "It's like I warned you, nobody's mind survives the Screaming Room for long."

"Cuticle mystery," Fernie declared, with special angry emphasis.

Gnulbotz didn't try to talk to her much after that, but instead chuckled to himself every once in a while, whenever Fernie twitched and spat out a *"Liquid screwdriver"* or *"Elementary penguin,"* just to keep up the illusion. She took Hans Gloom's lead and let her mouth hang open so she could drool and murmur to herself and continue to look as thoroughly demented as possible.

She almost dropped the ploy when the dark corridor they traveled joined another, and Gnulbotz's platoon of guards met another led by a hulking shadow with a pair of the smelliest feet Fernie had ever encountered. Other guards carried shadow prisoners in glass jars, and led human prisoners on leashes, and while Fernie could not tell who the shadow prisoners were because they didn't look like anything more than swirling clouds of darkness on their side of the glass, she had no trouble recognizing Not-Roger, her sister, and her father.

As much as Fernie's heart soared at the sight, and as much as she wanted to weep with happiness while crying out their names, she forced herself to maintain her blank-eyed, slack-jawed expression. "Why, who are these other *neon centipedes?*"

Mr. What struggled to break free of his leash. "Fernie! What's wrong with you? Don't you recognize us?"

Gnulbotz showed his nasty teeth, filled with little squirming creatures. "Don't waste your time, fool. Her mind's been completely destroyed by the Screaming Room."

"No!" Mr. What cried. "I refuse to believe it! Speak to me, Fernie! Tell me that's still you in there!"

Gnulbotz cackled. "I tell you, you should save yourselves the effort. She doesn't remember any part of her previous life."

Fernie rolled her eyes at her father, managing a wink she could only hope he noticed, as she steered her insane gibberish toward references her father and sister might recognize. "*Fluorescent Salmon house. Safety expert father. Famous adventurer mother. Frankenstein monster-head slippers. Harrington's noogums.*"

In the silence that followed, Gnulbotz beamed with contentment. "See? I told you. Not one word of that made any sense at all."

"And furthermore," Fernie said, *"safety railings."*

Pearlie got it first. She bit back what threatened to become one of the widest grins of her young life, and managed to plaster a grief-stricken grimace on her face instead.

Then Mr. What figured it out, too. He cried, "Oh, my poor daughter!" He had never been a particularly good actor, and his attempt at a display of grief was a fine explanation for his failure to get cast in any of the community theater productions for which he'd ever auditioned. But none of the guards seemed to notice.

Fernie went on mumbling nonsense and rolling her head insanely as the shadow guards led her family up a flight of stairs, outside, and onto walkways very much like the castle walls she and her fellow prisoners had been forced to walk earlier. As before, some of the courtyards below remained crowded with prisoners both human and shadow, penned into spaces too small for them. Another was now the cage of a gnarfle, happily munching away as one screaming shadow after another slid into its pen on a chute. Yet another looked like a pool of filthy water, except that shadow faces kept rising through the murk and crying for release before tentacles from below wrapped around them and pulled them back down. Fernie ached to ask questions about these and some of the other things she saw, but asking a question that made sense would have ruined her current disguise as a crazy person, so she refrained, hoping Pearlie or her dad would ask those questions for her. Unfortunately, neither one of them seemed to be in the mood to ask questions.

Then she spotted their apparent destination, a vast platform the size of a football field, balanced on what appeared to be the outermost wall of the castle, upon which a large number of faceless shadows and human servants of Lord Obsidian stood together. The dozens of humans were scarred and lumpy folks of the sort who looked like they were held together by their collection of dirt. They were all equipped with swords, though their smiles made it clear that the same could not be said of teeth. There were just as many shadows, all figures like Krawg and Gnulbotz, beings who seemed to take being disgusting as a matter of personal pride.

One being taller than all the rest, by about the height of a house, stood in their center, and Fernie's heart skipped a beat when she recognized the face in the center of the crescent-shaped head as a version of the one that had once belonged to a man named Howard Philip October. He made his way through the crowd, idly brushing one of his long misshapen hands on the shoulder of one of his human guards on the way, and that human shuddered and withered and fell to the ground as a dry husk, in the course of less than a second.

Fernie wanted to cry out in horror, as her father and sister were, but that would have revealed that her mind was still working, so she simply flashed a goofy grin and exclaimed, *"Moo cows!"*

Hans Gloom said nothing about what they had witnessed, but instead murmured something just as insane.

Lord Obsidian did not emerge from the crowd alone. He moved with two other figures familiar to Fernie.

To Lord Obsidian's left stood Gustav Gloom, whose impeccable black suit was now a tattered and frayed version of its usual self. It was impossible to tell from his unsmiling lips or serious eyes just what was going through his mind. He might have been grim and he might have been defeated, and he might have been simply biding his time; it was hard to tell. He showed no sign of being glad to see the What girls and their father. His eyes did seem to widen a little bit when he saw his own father for the very first time in his life, but then they returned to their previous heavy-lidded condition, and there was once again no sign that he was even paying attention.

To Lord Obsidian's right—and straining at his leash like a bad dog—crouched a monster that Fernie remembered with dread from their prior encounters in Gustav's house. It was the Beast, it was vicious, and when it saw Fernie, it tensed, eager to leap at her and avenge its past humiliations.

Mr. What, who had been unconscious the last time he was so close to the creature, gasped. Pearlie, who had never caught more than a glimpse of it, did the same. Not-Roger, who as far as Fernie knew had never seen it at all before this moment, told nobody in particular, "See, that's the kind of thing that keeps people in the Dark Country from thinking it's unreasonable to keep hungry gnarfles as pets."

A guard slapped the back of his head to silence him.

A final familiar face, Scrofulous, stepped out of the crowd, produced a scroll, and read aloud: "Attention, insignificant gnats! You have all been summoned to face the judgment of his unparalleled magnificence, the greatest and most underappreciated genius ever produced by the human race! Tremble at the very sight of the conqueror of the Dark Country and the future destroyer of the unworthy universe that existed before his arrival! He whose most rancid breath on the backs of our necks honors those of us whose lives have no meaning except for the honor we are paid by allowing ourselves to be crushed by him! The former Howard Philip October and current Lord Obsidian!"

He rolled up the scroll, glancing at his master for approval.

"Second rate," Lord Obsidian allowed, "but not quite as uninspired as the last introduction I had you whipped for."

"Thank you, Majesty. I do my best."

The towering Obsidian then peered past the cowering Scrofulous at the prisoners his minions had just brought him. "And you, my barely competent servants. You have brought the prisoners I requested? Not just the pathetic beings the boy came all this distance to save, but also those who provided him aid and comfort along the way?"

Gnulbotz performed a bow so deep that the top of his head almost touched the floor. "Aye, master. The girl, Fernie, and the man, Hans, have both lost their minds in the Screaming Room, but I brought them anyway, as well as a traitorous shadow who I found with them and brought to you in a jar."

Krawg attempted the same bow but caught a whiff of his own feet and almost passed out before recovering. "I have brought the girl's reportedly even tougher sister, Pearlie, their useless coward of a father, and the hulking fool from Shadow's Inn; also another handful of shadows with whom I found them conspiring and have also brought to you in jars."

Lord Obsidian offered a dismissive wave of his hand before advancing and lowering his crescent-shaped face to within a few inches of Hans Gloom's. He peered into his old enemy's eyes, tilting his own head first one way and then the next as he searched Gloom's staring eyes for signs of the enemy he had once known. "Fascinating," he said, at last. "The Screaming

Room did its job well. I see no sign of the man who once pursued me for so long and with so much heart. Once, I peered into these eyes and saw a world filled with oceans of love, deep wells of courage, and gardens of unexpected strength, but I have now razed all of that to the ground. Nothing is left but mountains of madness."

Mr. What asked him, "Is that the kind of thing that makes you proud of yourself?"

The crescent-shaped head tilted again, focusing the full force of Lord Obsidian's glare at him. "Why, yes. Thanks for asking."

Mr. What's mouth dropped open as if he dearly wanted to retort, but dared not.

Obsidian rose to his full height, towering over his followers and his servants and his prisoners, his broken-glass voice echoing in the cold Dark Country air. "But you must all wonder why I have taken time out of my busy schedule to have my greatest enemy and all of these other troublesome prisoners brought to my side.

"The halfsie boy, Gustav Gloom, has foolishly informed me that he believes there to be a bright side in every situation, no matter how dire—even this one. He is wrong.

"This is not his fault. He's just a foolish little boy, and the universe as I see it is a cold, pitiless place, beyond the comprehension of foolish little boys. There is no room for hope in it.

"He claims to have found satisfaction in destroying the statues in my throne room. It is a pale and pathetic thing, but it nevertheless allows him comfort, and so I shall destroy that one source of hope, while forcing his friends to watch."

Fernie's heart had fallen further with every word. Lord Obsidian was so confident, so assured in what he said he wanted to do, that it almost felt like he'd already succeeded in building the hopeless universe he envisioned. As much as she could without looking like she was sane and capable of focusing on other people, she searched Gustav's face for some sign that he had a plan capable of preventing Lord Obsidian from doing any of the things he claimed he could. But though she had learned a lot about reading his usual facial expressions in the time she'd been his best friend, she saw nothing in his eyes now but emptiness and defeat.

Is this it? she wondered.

Have we really lost?

Or (and she was really grasping at straws here) was that little twitch of his eyebrows and that little curlicue wrinkle at the corner of his lips as close as Gustav could get to a reassuring smile without being caught?

She tried to focus on his face long enough to tell for sure, but whatever she thought she had seen was already gone.

Lord Obsidian returned to Mr. What and, cocking his crescent-moon-shaped head again, pointed outside the castle walls at the landscape's strangest feature, the two suspiciously round mountains whose summits were hidden behind all-concealing clouds.

"Do you know what you're looking at?" he inquired.

"Mountains?" Mr. What guessed.

"I would expect you to say that, because you're a silly unimaginative man with the vision of a newt. But yes, sir, mountains will do as a guess. Mountains as tall as the tallest anyone in your world of light has ever seen.

"But those are not mountains, sir. They are the smallest and least impressive parts of a magnificent statue, one that rises so far above our heads that all the works of man are proven insignificant by comparison.

"Are you willing to guess what they are now?"

Mr. What hesitated. "Am I allowed to guess?"

"I am ordering you to guess."

Mr. What struggled to come up with an answer. "Sorry. I've got nothing."

But Fernie remembered a sight she'd seen from the ridge that surrounded the Dark Country on all sides: a head that was as big as a mountain range all by itself, emerging out of the swirling murk.

She had always been the kind of girl who blurted out answers in class, and she now came very close to abandoning her disguise as a crazy person just to do the same thing.

The only reason she didn't was that Pearlie beat her to it. She sounded awed and horrified and as close to being without hope as Lord Obsidian wanted her to be, but she went ahead and said it: "That's the front of the giant statue's shoes!"

Lord Obsidian whirled toward Gustav, his pointed chin and forehead slashing through the air like knives. "Are your hopes shattered yet, boy? Do you see how much my achievements dwarf anything you could ever imagine?"

Gustav shut his eyes and shook his head, as if even the small part of the sculpture visible to him was more than his little mind could accept. His next words emerged as a whine. "They're just shoes . . ."

"Have you no vision, boy? They're just the smallest part of a statue that pierces the clouds!"

Gustav opened his mouth, as if struggling for words capable of reducing Lord Obsidian's proudest achievement to terms he could accept, but then he just shook his head again. He looked like a boy who had just lost everything but had yet to admit it to himself, and could only keep from falling apart by denying the very evidence of his own eyes. Fernie could not be sure his reaction was real, because part of her still hoped he was pretending like she was. But she could not stop her heart from breaking for him.

Gustav finally managed an even more pathetic whine. "Just shoes . . ."

"Bah," said Lord Obsidian. (He actually said "Bah" as if it were a word, which showed extreme misunderstanding of the sound villains and grumpy old men are really supposed to be making when books describe them as saying "Bah.") "I'll show you."

He waved the terrible fingers at the ends of his terrible hands, and the entire platform holding him and his minions and their various prisoners detached from the castle wall and began to rise . . .

CHAPTER TWELVE
A GRAND TOUR OF
A TYRANT'S SWELLED HEAD

Fernie felt the sudden jar as the platform started to rise, and cried out, which was a sane thing to do, but as all eyes, human and shadow, turned toward her, she quickly covered her sanity with a happy declaration of, "This is the most *typewriter fudge* I ever *Florida!*"

Hans Gloom also swayed with the sudden lurch, and for a moment dropped his own slack-jawed expression, but all of the guards were focusing on Fernie at that moment and none saw his brief look of determination. Pearlie also cried out, and Mr. What muttered something under his breath about the madness of building a flying machine without any safety railings or seat belts. The various human and shadow guards merely jostled, trying to stay as far away from its edges as they possibly could.

Gathering speed, the platform left Obsidian's

castle behind and drew closer to the giant shoes, which closer up revealed a frightening wealth of detail that included shoelaces tied into bows that must have been, themselves, the size of some entire neighborhoods back in the world of light.

The platform rose higher, into the shadowy mists that had up until now hidden the upper regions of the statue from view. However, this close to the statue, the mists failed to hide everything. The broad outlines of the giant version of Howard Philip October loomed before them, and though it must have still been many miles away, its sheer size remained terrifying. It took almost a minute for the platform to rise past the pair of colossal trouser cuffs, another couple of minutes for it to rise sufficiently high up the legs to pass the statue's knees, another minute for it to reach the distant outlines of a belt buckle.

"Imagine!" Lord Obsidian crowed. "Can you even conceive how many slaves, human and shadow, must have labored with aching backs and dripping brows, to further my glory?"

Fernie couldn't. She knew what slavery was, because she'd learned about it and read about it and even seen some movies about it. But it was impossible to look upon the giant version of

Howard Philip October and not feel the awfulness of it. Uncounted beings permitted no rights of their own had labored for so long, in some cases, just to construct a belt buckle that all by itself might have been the size of England.

Higher, and the statue's arm bent over its chest, holding a gigantic copy of one of October's books, *The Shadows From Before Time.*

Then the platform ascended above the Dark Country's awful murk. They found themselves facing the part of the statue that Fernie and her friends had seen before, at a much greater distance: the immense head that rose out of the clouds. But before, they had been many thousands of miles away from it. Now they were much closer to it, though even now perhaps as far as a hundred miles away. It filled the sky before them like a planet with a human face.

Howard Philip October's face, complete with his big jaw and big forehead and an expression of determined nobility that existed nowhere in the petty monster the man had been, rose before them.

It was too much for a mere human mind to take in all at once. Without knowing it, Fernie had fallen to her knees. She glanced over her shoulder and, through a haze of tears, saw that Pearlie and

Not-Roger and her father had all collapsed as well, unable to accept the terrible immensity of Lord Obsidian's monument to himself.

Even the Beast, crouched at its master's side, whined because of it.

Far worse, though, was the realization that Gustav Gloom had also been destroyed by the sight. He curled into a ball and shook silently, as if there were sobs within him that no amount of denial could keep in. "P-please," he said, his voice breaking. "Land. Land on the head. I can't look at it from a distance anymore."

"Very well," Lord Obsidian said kindly. "Now that you're broken, and fit for a miserable lifetime as my servant, I can afford to be generous with you."

He waved his terrible hands another time, and the platform changed course. Despite the speed it must have been traveling, there was no wind, no sense of motion; just that giant head continuing to grow closer before them.

Soon they passed over the great balding scalp, and the landscape before them was no longer recognizable as the sculpture of a human being, but instead resembled a vast and forbidding desert, great enough to qualify as a country all by itself.

The platform skimmed low over the balding top of the head for a while. The statue was so big that from this angle it was impossible to see anything but an immense plain, flat on top but with a subtle downward curve toward each horizon. Towering arcs of what Fernie supposed were hair formed a forest of sorts in the distance, but they were miles away, reflecting how far up his scalp October's hairline had receded by the time he became the man pictured on the back cover of his books. It was probably best for a smooth landing that Lord Obsidian steered the platform toward a spot closer to the bald part of his scalp.

The platform descended and settled, coming to rest only one short step up from the stone surface beneath it. For a second or two the gathered humans and shadows glanced at one another, wondering what to do. Then Gustav made a sound very much like a sob and ran from them, leaping off the edge of the platform and running into the stone desert as quickly as his little legs could carry him.

Fernie dared to hope that this was part of some brilliant plan, but was disappointed almost immediately, because Gustav traveled fewer than fifty paces before he fell to his hands and knees again, trembling.

Some of the human guards readied their spears and started to go after him.

"No," said Lord Obsidian, with the annoyance of a movie fan who didn't want somebody else to spoil a good one by telling him how it was all going to work out. "There is no need."

Gustav remained where he'd fallen. He had stopped shaking the way Fernie and Pearlie and Mr. What and Hans Gloom and even Not-Roger were shaking, but he didn't look like he had any fight left in him, either.

Lord Obsidian noted this. "Behold, my friends. The child of my greatest enemy, broken before us. Reduced to hopelessness in front of all the foolish friends and allies who followed him to this, the moment of his defeat. It is the greatest triumph of my life."

Fernie felt the floodgates let loose. Through a fog of tears she looked back at her father and at Pearlie, who had each been let loose by their respective guards and were now huddled together grimly, having lost all hope as well. She wished there was something she could say to them. But she had no words left.

Lord Obsidian, on the other hand, had plenty. He spun in place, like a child excited by a carnival, his elongated fingers slashing the air like swords. He cried, "Is this not magnificent? Look on my works, ye mighty, and despair!"

Fernie realized that she'd been wrong about believing her minute exposed to the full effect of the Screaming Room to be the worst point of her life. *This* was the worst point of her life. There was no hope left. Sunlight had vanished from the universe. All around her, everybody seemed to feel it—not just the prisoners, but also Lord Obsidian's followers, who, in the wake of their master's command to abandon all hope, seemed prepared to do just that.

Nobody said a word. Nobody breathed.

And then, still on his hands and knees, Gustav muttered, "That's not the point of the poem."

Lord Obsidian whirled. "What is this?"

Gustav sat up, dusted off his pants with slaps of his palms, and then turned around and peered across the expanse of stone to the crowd on the platform.

He winked when he spotted Fernie, and sunlight, glorious sunlight, returned to her heart at once.

Then he faced Lord Obsidian from across the not-nearly-sufficient distance that separated them, and cocked his head. "You heard me the first time, Howie. That's not the point of the poem."

"What are you talking about?"

"What you just said about how we should all look upon your works and despair. I know you were a writer once, but I'm a reader. I know that you didn't come up with that line all by yourself. It actually comes from a very old and very famous poem by a guy named Percy Shelley."

"'Ozymandias,'" Mr. What whispered. He must have known the poem, too . . . and it must have meant something to him, because just remembering it was enough to bring a wild hope into his voice.

Fernie didn't know the poem herself, because she'd never really gone for poetry, and the only one she'd ever liked at all was a really creepy one about a weird guy being pestered by a talkative black bird. But she could sense the power balance shifting in a way that might soon give all of them a split second's fighting chance . . . so she rose to her feet, daring to believe, readying herself for anything.

Lord Obsidian had taken a single step, as if intent on tearing the boy limb from limb, but something stopped him before he advanced any farther: perhaps just irritation, and perhaps just curiosity . . . but perhaps another emotion, one that it was probably not good for a would-be conqueror to have. "Explain yourself, boy."

"Sure thing, Howie." Gustav cracked his knuckles. "See, in the poem you quoted, those words, *Look on my works*, and so on, are found on the pedestal of another statue, a shattered statue, built a long time ago by another big bully who also once wanted everybody to be afraid of him. But in the poem, the statue's in ruins. The rest has all crumbled. His kingdom's gone, his dreams of conquest are dead, and the man himself is forgotten. The point of the poem is that he was a big deal for a little while, but he ended up with nothing."

Lord Obsidian almost seemed relieved. "And that's your big plan? Finger-wagging based on some words from some foolish poet long dead?"

Gustav suddenly looked very tired. He rubbed the bridge of his nose and said, "You know, Howie, you really are an idiot sometimes."

The words rippled through the crowd, humans and shadows nudging one another, demanding to know: *Did he really say that?*

Gustav went on. "Do you really think we'd all be parked in this particular spot right now if I hadn't *wanted* us to get here all along?"

His words, gently as he spoke them, hit with the force of a thunderbolt. The human guards elbowed one another, unsure what to do. The shadows murmured. Scrofulous peered from face to face and seemed to remember the promise Gustav had made to him earlier. The Beast whined and cowered and snarled, eager for a chance to attack.

Mr. What gave his astonished shadow guard a nasty look, then scooped up Pearlie and, without meeting any resistance at all, went to Fernie, proud to stand beside his daughters.

Mr. Gloom dropped the look of bereft madness from his face and took a step closer, his eyes welling with something more than hope.

Though still towering in their midst, and still the most dangerous shadow in sight, Lord Obsidian clearly sensed that he was now in danger of no longer being seen as the most dangerous person at this gathering. He snarled, "You're lying."

Gustav turned his attention back to Fernie. "Are you okay?"

Fernie's voice broke. "I'm f-fine. I was only pretending to be crazy."

Gnulbotz whirled toward her, his eyes widening in shock, and the many squirming little maggots in his mouth all rearing back as if personally offended.

Gustav's lip twitched. "Really, Fernie, being a little bit crazy is one of the things I like most about you."

"Being a little bit crazy," she said, grinning through her tears, "is probably also the reason I like you, too."

Gustav's lips quivered with one of his many barely-a-smile smiles. He then turned to Lord Obsidian and asked him, "So, Howie, would you like to know why you've just made the second biggest mistake of your life? I realize we're about to fight to the death, but if you really want to know, I'm in no hurry. I can spare a minute or so to tell you."

Lord Obsidian was positively trembling with fury. "You have my permission to speak, boy. But every word you say now will invite even-more-protracted suffering for yourself later."

"Whatever," said Gustav, who was clearly not impressed.

He started to pace.

"See, Howie, I've read every single one of your books. There are copies of all of them in my home library. I've had years to study every page, trying to figure out what kind of awful person would do the kind of things you've done.

"They're really not very good books.

"But one of the things I noticed about them was that while you were okay at describing things like otherworldly dimensions and ancient lost cities, you were pretty hopeless when it came to writing about people.

"Whenever you were forced to write about people, it was obvious that you didn't have even the slightest idea what you were talking about.

"Other people just weren't real to you, Howie. And I guess that much makes sense, because if other people did feel real to you, you wouldn't have done all the terrible things you've done to them, over the years."

Gustav shrugged. "Even growing up without people, I always knew more about them than you did. I don't know why. Maybe because I came from good people. Maybe because I always knew I was one of them, and you always thought you were above them.

"I've always known I would someday have a chance to use that against you.

"So when I was in your throne room, destroying all those statues of yourself you found so important, I made a point of telling you, again and again, how silly I found them. I said it so many times that you had to get irritated. I wanted you to be irritated.

"Then I told you how much satisfaction I took in destroying them all . . . and you got so irritated you have done exactly what I wanted. You brought me *here*."

Gustav let the meaning of those words sink in, and a large number of Lord Obsidian's guards and soldiers looked around nervously, already seeing how those words would indeed lead their master to bring the boy to this one place.

None of them saw why this place would be more dangerous for their master than any other place, but they all heard the confidence in Gustav's voice, the sense that the tide had just turned.

Fernie understood more. She remembered the last thing Gustav had said to Lemuel Gloom's shadow, when sending him away with the Cryptic Carousel. Gustav had told him to take the vehicle somewhere safe, and wait for a signal—a signal he didn't have enough information to explain yet, but which he had promised to make sure Lemuel could spot from the air above the Dark Country.

The statue's head was the only feature of the Dark Country that could be seen above its thick, roiling murk.

It was, she understood with mounting excitement, the only place in the entire land from which a distress signal could be sent.

Gustav went on. "I knew that a guy like you wouldn't ever be able to resist breaking my spirit by bringing me to the most impressive statue you had, the one I'd already seen from a distance.

"Seriously, Howie. You were so easy to manipulate that I almost felt sorry for you. I didn't even have to say all that much more after that, to get you to think that sending for all my captive friends and family was your own good idea instead of mine.

"You never knew it was because that would save me the trouble of running around looking for them after I got finished kicking your butt."

Gustav spread his hands, palms outward. "And so here we are, exactly where I wanted us to be: the place where I'll finish the job my father started." His gaze darted briefly toward Hans Gloom, whose face now radiated so much pride in his son that the shadow soldiers all around him looked even darker in comparison to his shining light. "That is, if it's okay with you, Dad."

Hans Gloom's voice broke. "You're doing fine all by yourself . . . son."

Lord Obsidian's face whipped toward the man he had long considered his greatest enemy, the man he had believed to be a broken shell. Fury stained his gray features, but there was even more uncertainty now, even more fear . . . and in that moment, there was not a single being on the platform who failed to see it.

Then he turned back to Gustav and snarled, "I commend you, boy. You are too conniving to trust as a servant. You would clearly just find some way to push me aside and rule in my stead. So I will just have to kill you and all your friends. But before I do, you need to clear up the one thing you left unexplained. You called bringing you here the *second* biggest mistake of my life. What, in your foolish opinion, was my first?"

Gustav had already reached into the remains of his jacket and removed a small object. "Oh, that," he said. "You never should have killed Penny Gloom."

The object between his fingers was a whistle.

The next two things to happen occurred simultaneously.

First: Lord Obsidian snapped a command at the Beast. *"You! Kill the What family! Now!"*

And second: Gustav blew the whistle.

CHAPTER THIRTEEN
THE GREAT BATTLE BEGINS

The Beast, as always happiest now that it had somebody to attack, burst from Lord Obsidian's side and leaped at the three gathered members of the What family.

As it grew to fill the air before them, it changed from its usual awful self to something even more awful, all mouth and claws and swirling darkness. It was so horrid in its outline that even the shadow guards cringed in sudden terror at the sight of it.

Fernie had been able to outrun the monster in the past, but never without a tremendous head start.

She cried out, firmly expecting this to be the very last second of her life.

Then something flung her and Pearlie aside at the last instant. They went flying, sprawling onto the platform floor.

Fernie landed hard, scraping her knees, realizing even as she skidded to a stop that it had been her father who shoved her and Pearlie out of the Beast's path, placing himself between them and danger.

She cried out, *"No, Dad—"*

But even as she rolled over on her back to face what she had firmly expected to be the most horrible of all sights, another surprise awaited her.

The Beast was not ripping her father apart, but instead rising into the air at the end of a lasso.

The lasso was a cable hanging from the base of a colorful merry-go-round that had suddenly materialized in the air over them.

She cried out, "The Cryptic Carousel!"

It was indeed the marvelous vehicle invented by Gustav's grandfather Lemuel.

In the next second it gave a sudden violent spin, the carousel animals turning into streaks of bright color and the lassoed Beast becoming a foul gray blur circling the carnival ride at the end of its rope.

Then the Cryptic Carousel released the line, and the lassoed Beast went flying off into the far distance, its furious roar growing ever more faint as it became a dot dropping into the murk from a height.

Pearlie said, "Well, that much was easy, at least."

The calliope music the carousel played cut out, and the amplified voice of Lemuel Gloom's shadow boomed through the high-altitude air: *"Now!"*

The robotic carousel animals, designed to provide defense and protection for the strange vehicle's passengers, now did their job, leaping away from their respective poles and into the midst of the enemy.

Whinnying, the carousel unicorn speared two shadow guards and ran off into the distance, with them still squirming together on its horn.

Roaring, the carousel lion took on three of the human guards and backed them off with its slashing claws.

The carousel salmon tumbled from the sky, mouth-first, and swallowed one guard up to the waist, leaving him stumbling around on confused legs while the fish thrashed on top of him.

The carousel zebra, rhino, ostrich, and octopus-man hit the platform, right into a knot of screaming and confused minions, scattering them like bowling pins.

The battle was already far too complicated for Fernie to understand all at once, but she saw little puzzle pieces of it that, if she survived, she might be able to fit into some kind of sense later.

As far as she could tell, all of this took place at the same moment:

Not-Roger lifted a squirming human guard over his head and flung him at two others, bowling them over.

Scrofulous wandered about in the midst of the chaos, clutching his scroll and muttering to himself, "Oh dear, oh dear, oh dear . . ."

Mr. What picked up an abandoned sword and touched his fingertip to the end of it, immediately wincing and drawing it back with the kind of thoughtful expression that he always wore when doing his job as a safety expert, possibly figuring out some kind of safeguard that could be added to a sword to make sure it couldn't ever accidentally cut anybody.

Hans Gloom ripped his leash away from his guards, placed a hand on the shoulder of a guard facing the other way, turned the man around, and socked him in the jaw, knocking him down.

Gustav raced toward the battle, yelling, "Dad!"

The Cryptic Carousel dove for the crowd, forcing shadows and humans alike to cry out and dive for the floor.

The carousel rhino rammed one of the shadow guards, knocking him over and making him lose his grip on the glass jar he held. It shattered on the ground, freeing a dark cloud of mist that first became a frightened Anemone, then blurred, shifted shape, and re-emerged as a grim-faced Great-Aunt Mellifluous.

Lord Obsidian cried out in rage and advanced through the chaos, making a beeline for his old enemy, Hans Gloom.

All of that happened in *one second*.

So many things of similar craziness happened in the *next* second that neither Fernie nor Pearlie knew where they should go themselves to make the most helpful contribution.

Their father gave his recently acquired sword an experimental swing, just to see how it felt, and without realizing it, cut an advancing Krawg in half. "Sorry," he said automatically, though he probably wasn't. Krawg re-formed, and Mr. Gloom cut him in half again, getting used to the idea.

Gnulbotz tried to grab Gustav, only to close his hands on empty air as the boy leaped through his grasp.

Lord Obsidian extended his grotesquely elongated fingers toward Hans Gloom, but one of his human servants got in the way, and Obsidian grasped him by mistake. The man screamed and aged about eighty years in a heartbeat, finally crumbling into a pile of ash. Obsidian dropped him and slashed at

Hans, who evaded him and dove through the crowd, trying to find a sword he could use.

A dozen of the remaining shadow guards converged on the shouting Great-Aunt Mellifluous, swarming her in numbers so great that in less than a second she disappeared from view.

Not-Roger grabbed a fallen human guard by one arm and one leg and spun him in circles, using him to drive away half a dozen others.

Three of the shadow guards slipped away from the chaos, cradling their glass jars. A carousel zebra brushed one and caused him to drop his charge, which shattered and released a cloud of darkness that immediately re-formed into Pearlie's shadow.

Pearlie cried, "Who do we help first?"

Fernie yelled, "No time to make plans! Just do whatever makes the most sense!"

Even as the girls entered the battle, an angry Lord Obsidian stormed through it all, calling his guards fools and brushing them aside in his determination to deal with Hans Gloom. Each human guard he brushed aside crumbled into ashes at his touch, demonstrating the chief risk of working for world-conquering maniacs: They don't repay their followers' loyalty with any of their own. The human guards who saw what Lord Obsidian was doing screamed and ran, less interested in quelling the revolt than they were in keeping away from their master's touch.

Hans scrambled across the platform floor on his hands and knees, at one point darting between the legs of the carousel's winged horse. He emerged on the other side to find himself facing an angry human guard charging him with a spear. Hans grabbed the spear behind its point, jabbed the guard in the face with its handle, and claimed the weapon for himself. He spun it in his hands and brandished it at Lord Obsidian, who had simply stepped over the winged horse in a single step and now glared down at his old enemy with the booming arrogance of a giant facing down a child.

Gustav raced through the crowd, desperate to get to the father he had never known.

Pearlie and her shadow attacked one of the human guards protecting a jar. Pearlie dove to grab him by his ankles, at the same time her shadow tried to wrest away the jar. The guard turned to avoid Pearlie's shadow but got his legs twisted up by Pearlie's grip. He fell face-first. The jar sailed through the air, hit the ground, and shattered into a million pieces. Another cloud of swirling darkness popped out and re-formed itself. Penny Gloom's shadow whirled about to find either her strange son or the man she had spent so many years loving and protecting.

Fernie found herself facing a filthy human guard, clad in chain-mail shorts, who jabbed his rusted sword at her face and said, "At least I'll get to kill one of ye for the master!"

She ducked under his sword, yanked his chain-mail shorts down around his ankles, and ran past him while he was still stumbling about trying to figure out what had just happened.

Up ahead, Lord Obsidian wrapped his terrible hands around the spear wielded by Hans Gloom, and coldly snapped it in half. "First, you! Then the interfering brats!"

Above them all, the Cryptic Carousel rose back into the air, tilted like a hat worn at a jaunty angle. It now was crawling with shadow and human minions of Lord Obsidian who had managed to grab on during its dive and were struggling to board so they could seize control of the vehicle.

The carousel gorilla, an old friend of Fernie's, was the only carousel animal still aboard and not directly involved with the battle below. He stomped and kicked at the minions clinging to the carousel's side, but could use only one arm because he needed to keep a certain familiar cat carrier tucked under his other.

Harrington's spitting and yowling could be heard even over the shouting of the mob. He was not a happy cat, though it was impossible to know, if he were free, whether he would have found some place to hide or joined the battle himself.

Gustav, leaping on and diving off the charging carousel rhino's back, knocked his father to the ground and away from Lord Obsidian's grasp.

Both the younger and the elder Gloom scrambled into the busiest part of the confusion, leaving Obsidian spinning in place as he searched for somebody more convenient to kill.

Unfortunately, the tyrant spotted Fernie.

Fernie had faced down a number of monsters of late, and had, until now, imagined she was getting used to it; but not that face, not those eyes. They were the eyes of a creature who had never felt a moment of genuine warmth for anything that lived, whose only reaction to anything good was the need to destroy it. An evil smile spread across his elongated, crescent features, as he said, "Yes. I should take the very smallest one first and work my way up to greater pleasures."

He reached for her.

Everything else in the battle faded into the background as those impossibly long fingers stretched toward her. Behind him, the shadows falling from the carousel became a kind of slow-motion rain, so far away that they might have come from another planet.

Then there was a sudden flash of steel as a heavy sword slammed against Lord Obsidian's knuckles with an audible clang. It didn't sever any of Obsidian's fingers and probably damaged the sword more than his hand, but it did knock the giant hand aside just before its deadly touch would have brushed Fernie's cheeks.

Stung, Lord Obsidian clutched that hand with the other and stepped back to behold who would have dared do such an impudent thing.

Mr. What stood alone, the smoking sword in front of him, looking like a man who had absolutely no idea what he was expected to do next but was willing to do it anyway.

Fernie could hardly believe her eyes. "Dad?"

Lord Obsidian looked even more astonished. "You? You're the most pathetic of all of them! A terrified little man who lives his life in fear, imagining ways to protect himself from all the world's imagined dangers!"

"Not just myself," Mr. What said, "and not just imagined. Fernie, get behind me."

Horrified by what she saw about to happen, Fernie protested: "You can't fight *him*, Dad. Not with a *sword*!"

Mr. What didn't waver one instant. "I'd rather be anywhere else, doing any*thing* else, Fernie, but nobody ever asked me for my vote, and I *am* your father. Get behind me, young lady. Now."

Fernie would have protested further, but then something grabbed her by the wrist and pulled her away.

Above her head, the carousel went into another high-speed spin, scattering shadows and humans in all directions. Elsewhere, Not-Roger let go of the man he was swinging and sent him flying over the crowd with a scream that became just another of many filling the gray air. Pearlie broke the jar containing Not-Roger's shadow, and he burst free, leaping into the crowd of enemy shadows with a roaring battle cry. Gustav and Hans Gloom grabbed swords and fought side by side, wearing identical fierce expressions on faces that were impossible to avoid seeing as linked by heredity. There was shouting and running and fighting everywhere. But Fernie, being pulled away by the whisper-soft hand of Great-Aunt Mellifluous, had no eyes for anything but her father, thin and small and armed with nothing but a puny sword, but standing resolute against an amazed enemy the size of a house.

Mr. What lifted that sword to block another blow from Lord Obsidian's fingers, and though he succeeded in parrying Obsidian's hit, was knocked to one knee by the force of it. He managed to rise back to his feet and shouted at the towering figure above him: "Is that the best you can do, you ugly freak? Come on!"

Fernie was desperate to pull free to help him. But Great-Aunt Mellifluous spun her around and knelt before her, cupping her cheeks. "There's no *time*, dear. Obsidian's forces must already know what's happening here, and are likely sending reinforcements from the castle even now. You need to get to the carousel and—"

A shadow guard bowled into Great-Aunt Mellifluous, knocking her away from Fernie.

The guard was a shape-changer who had made himself into a creature a lot like a gnarfle, with little stubby legs, little grasping hands, and a head that was mostly angry gnashing mouth. Great-Aunt Mellifluous fell to the ground beneath him, but she started to blur at once, shifting from her familiar old-woman guise, to the much slighter Anemone, to something that was in less than a second just as monstrous as the shape she fought.

"The armies!" she cried, for Fernie's benefit. "If we can't signal our own, then all is—"

Whatever else she had to say was cut off when she and the guard got all tangled up together and became something that looked like two storm clouds battling each other.

Fernie was pretty sure that Gustav's great-aunt's next word would have been "lost."

She looked for her father. She saw that Lord Obsidian had reached down and touched the tip of Mr. What's sword with one of his great distorted fingers. The part of the blade that remained visible, just before the hilt, was already turning yellow and tarnished with age.

Mr. What still held on grimly, shouting something Fernie couldn't hear. He seemed like he had doubled in size, and she had trouble telling why until she saw that another shadow surrounded him, adding to his grip with the strength of his own arms. It was recognizable as her father's shadow only because it did everything her father was doing, but in outline it was bulkier, more muscled, looking like her father might have looked if he'd lived the life of a great warrior, renowned wherever he went for his fearlessness and strength.

Without understanding how, Fernie suddenly knew that it was the shadow of the man her father had always been, for all his constant fussing and worrying about safety.

He'd never been frightened of anything, not really. He'd just been careful.

But even with his shadow's help, her father was still losing.

As the blade crumbled, a grinning Lord Obsidian moved his fingertip closer to the hilt, taking obvious pleasure in the inevitability of his enemy's defeat.

Fernie's father had only seconds left . . .

. . . but Great-Aunt Mellifluous had told her she needed to get to the carousel.

. . . but Fernie was the only one who even saw the trouble he was in.

. . . but there was nothing she could do herself to save him from Lord Obsidian.

. . . but he was *Dad*.

. . . but . . .

Fernie made the hardest decision she'd ever had to make in her life and, rather than rushing to help her father, she ran in another direction, twisting away from the various evil hands trying to grab her, and heading straight for the only thing she'd seen today that could possibly be able to help.

She found herself in the path of the charging unicorn. There were already what looked like two dozen shadow soldiers impaled on its horn, struggling to get free. They would survive the experience, but Fernie had no reason to believe she would, so she evaded its charge and ran toward one of the sprawled human guards. This fellow looked like he had already had more than enough of the fighting. His head, which lay facedown in front of her on the platform, was bald and lumpy and bruised.

Building up as much speed as she could, Fernie used his back as a ramp, and his rather large and protruding butt as the closest thing she had to a trampoline.

It was the only way she could achieve enough height to do what she needed to do, and even then, she wasn't at all sure she would make it.

It was a near thing. A very near thing.

But she landed on the spot she'd aimed for.

Right in the saddle of the carousel's winged horse.

CHAPTER FOURTEEN
LORD OBSIDIAN SHOWS A DEGREE OF PERSONAL IRRITATION

The winged horse was so startled by the sudden weight on its back that it reared, trying to throw her off. But Fernie was prepared for that and held on to its mane, shouting, "Stop! Stop! You know me! *I'm one of the carousel's passengers!*"

The winged horse flapped its giant wings, scattering the vicious shadow minions around them. The act made it leave the ground, and for a moment it seemed about to settle again when Fernie cried, "No! No! You need to go up! I need to get back to the carousel right away!"

"But all the fun's down here," the winged horse complained.

The carousel's gorilla was capable of speech, and so Fernie was only mildly surprised that this animal came equipped with the same feature. "You'll be able to hurt them a lot more if you get me back to the carousel."

"This better be good," it warned as it rose into the air. "It's been years since I've been given a chance to get involved in a good fight."

Spreading its wings, the winged horse swooped low over the crowd, knocking over a handful of human guards who had been advancing on Hans and Gustav Gloom, and giving the father and son a moment's freedom to race to Mr. What's rescue.

Nor were they alone. Even as Hans and Gustav struggled to make their way across the battlefield, many more of their allies had rushed to help the bespectacled man who had taken on Lord Obsidian alone. Penny's shadow and Not-Roger's shadow and even Pearlie's shadow had all gathered behind her father's shadow, surrounding him and adding their strength to his as he struggled to wrest his rapidly disintegrating sword from Lord Obsidian's touch.

Mr. What had the look of a man who would have preferred being anywhere else in the universe, even on a Ferris wheel—and, really, for anyone who knew him, that was saying a lot. But he clung to the sword and refused to let go.

Fernie didn't really have time to try to save him, but even with her own important mission to complete, she couldn't ignore her father's plight anymore. She shouted an instruction to the winged horse, which dipped in mid-flight and gave Lord Obsidian a powerful kick in the head as it passed by. It was the kind of kick that might have pulped a watermelon, and Lord Obsidian was currently solid enough to feel it, but it didn't seem to hurt him much. He roared, but more in indignation than pain . . . and he didn't lose his grip on the blade.

Another loop, and she saw Not-Roger, who had picked up yet another human guard by the ankle and now had two he was swinging around like hammers. He cried up at her, joyfully, "You know what, Fernie? I think I used to do this kind of thing a lot!"

Fernie also flew over Pearlie, still alive and chasing the shadow minion who was trying to escape the battle with the last of the glass jars in his arms. It wasn't hard to figure out that the one shadow ally who still remained imprisoned was the mysterious Caliban. Fernie considered making another side trip to help Pearlie free him. But no. She'd already lost too much time.

The carousel filled the sky before her, spinning too quickly to be seen as anything but a colorful blur. As fast as it was moving, not just in its own circles but back and forth across the battlefield, sweeping away as many shadows as it could, a safe landing seemed impossible. Fernie almost closed her eyes to avoid seeing the crash that would most likely kill her. But just as she was certain she was about to die, all sense of movement vanished and she found herself sitting on a carousel animal that had taken its place in the circle and frozen there, once again mounted on its pole.

"Did you think I was going to crash?" the winged horse inquired. "Please. I learned how to land on a moving target long ago."

Fernie supposed it appropriate to say this much: "Thank you."

"I hope so," it replied. "Every moment I stay here, I miss more of the fun."

Fernie hopped down onto a carousel floor that was right now empty of all its animals except for the one she'd just ridden, and the helpful gorilla, who loped up to her with Harrington's carrier still tightly clutched under his hairy arm.

Harrington was, unsurprisingly, very wide-eyed.

"Welcome back, miss," the gorilla said. "Will

you want your pet back now? He's been yowling most insistently."

"Not yet, thank you! But take care of him!"

Ignoring the view out the side of the carousel, which spun and tilted and blurred and in all other ways attempted to make her faint with dizziness, she ran past a forest of abandoned silver poles to the carousel's hub, where Grandpa Lemuel's shadow stood at the controls with transparent fingers darting back and forth like furious birds.

Lemuel's shadow was so busy that he didn't look up to greet her. "I was very glad to see all of you, Fernie. You were all out of touch for so long that I almost gave up hope."

She was glad to see him, too, but didn't have the time to give him the joyful hug she thought he deserved. "We're still going to lose unless you do something right away."

"Really? It looks like we're doing okay."

"I know. But Lord Obsidian has entire *armies* under the clouds . . . and there's no telling how many might be already on their way here to help him."

His friendly eyes darkened with concern. "Should I go fight those instead?"

"No. We have to get a message to all the

oppressed shadows on the other side, the ones who could be fighting with us but are either so beaten down they can't imagine winning, or don't know that this is their one chance to rise up."

"Like what?"

"Back when Gustav and I were first learning to fly this thing, we accidentally shrank ourselves to the size of a mote of dust. Do you remember how to do that?"

"Of course. The carousel has always been able to change its size. It's the only way to be sure that wherever you go, there'll always be a place to park it. But how could getting smaller possibly—"

Fernie said, "I'm afraid you're still not getting it."

Below, many of the human guards were either down or still trying to stay out of the way of the rampaging carousel animals. Most of the shadow soldiers were either scattered or busy trying to help their embattled comrades. Pearlie was still chasing the shadow guard trying to hold on to that last jar. Gustav and Hans Gloom were still racing to Mr. What's aid, but had both needed to stop and evade the sword thrusts of all the shadow guards who had massed to stop them.

Much of the battle on the statue's head now came down to a single frightened man and a few shadows refusing to back down from one of the greatest monsters who ever lived.

The last of Mr. What's blade crumbled into a whiff of rusty powder, and Mr. What himself fell flat on his back, staring up at a laughing figure many times his size.

Mr. What scrambled away on his back, trying to get out of Lord Obsidian's way, but the furious tyrant simply advanced on him, taking his time, uncaring. The shadows who'd been adding their strength to Mr. What's flew over his shoulders and attacked Lord Obsidian themselves, but the scowling villain merely batted them aside, one after the other. One blow sent Pearlie's shadow flying; the next sent Not-Roger's shadow flying; the third sent Penny's shadow flying. Pearlie's shadow returned and wrapped herself around Lord Obsidian's legs in a bid to trip him up, but he simply plucked her off and threw her away again.

Lord Obsidian just knelt and poised his giant hand over Mr. What's helpless form, stopping with one long and snakelike finger scarcely an inch from the tip of the man's nose. "This was the overrated boy's great plan? This petty act of . . . mischief? The sudden appearance of a flying machine?"

"Seemed . . . pretty good . . . to me . . . ," Mr. What wheezed.

"I'm almost tempted to let you live. It should amuse you to know that, even as we speak, I have sent some of my forces to the Gloom house to free your old friend the People Taker and all the prisoners in the Hall of Shadow Criminals. It would amuse me even more to see your reaction when they demonstrate they have done what I bade them, to bring your foolish wife here to join you and the girls as slaves in my mines."

Mr. What tried to get up, but the lightest touch from one of Obsidian's fingers to the center of his forehead sent him back down to the cold ground. It had not been enough of a touch to suck the life from him, but he had clearly felt that terrible draining sensation, because his face had lost all its color, and he looked unlikely to get up even if Lord Obsidian had any intention of allowing him.

Obsidian stepped on his chest and pinned

him with the weight of his foot. "But no. I am now angry enough to kill. So first, you. Then the other worthless father. Then the boy. Then your brats. Your wife, when she arrives, can labor as a slave alone."

His fingers started to close on Mr. What's face . . .

The ground lurched.

It was like an earthquake, except that this was not Earth and, considering what the ground they were fighting on really was, the only thing the disturbance could possibly be called was a giant stone Howard Philip October head-quake.

A deafening vibration, like a jackhammer on pavement, except a thousand times worse, filled the air and sent all the humans, whether working for Lord Obsidian or fighting for the side of Gustav and the Whats, to their knees, clutching their ears in pain.

Everybody stumbled, even the carousel animals and shadows. Even Lord Obsidian himself, who drew his hand away from the fortunate Mr. What and staggered backward, demanding, "What's happening?"

Pearlie stumbled and dropped the jar she'd managed to wrest from the shadow minion's clutches. It shattered when it hit the stone, releasing a black cloud that immediately congealed into the shape of the hooded Caliban.

The shaking grew worse, almost like the surface they all fought on was ripping itself apart. Pearlie toppled to the ground, the shaking of the stone beneath her so violent that she bounced up and down as she tried to crawl back toward the center of the fight.

Over the next few seconds it became clear that there was now another sound, even louder than the grinding and quaking. It sounded like a distant hum, and then it became a louder hum, and then it became millions or possibly even billions of voices, shouting from every corner of the Dark Country as something impossible happened to the statue that towered at the center of that land.

Even this high above the Dark Country, they sounded like cries of terror from Lord Obsidian's followers . . . and cheers from his enemies.

Gustav gazed past the unsteady figure of Lord Obsidian and saw something happening at the stone head's horizon. At first it looked like an impossible storm, a reverse blizzard of boulders the size of flying hills, all being flung upward in the distance. This was followed by a swiftly spinning riot of color he recognized as the curve of the Cryptic Carousel, rising over that horizon as if it were a sun climbing to greet a new day.

But this was far too big to be the Cryptic Carousel.

This was what the Cryptic Carousel would have looked like if it ever happened to grow as large as a mountain.

"No!" Lord Obsidian screamed. "Not my statue! Not my beautiful statue!"

Gustav flashed the sunniest grin of his entire life, because he'd just figured out who was responsible.

"Fernie," he said, with sincere admiration. "You really *do* know how to make a beautiful mess . . ."

CHAPTER FIFTEEN
FACE-OFF ABOVE THE DARK COUNTRY

The spinning Cryptic Carousel, now the same diameter as the giant sculpted head on the Howard Philip October statue, had the same effect on the statue's face that an industrial sander would have had on any other ugly lump.

Standing at the control panel, Lemuel's shadow remarked, "I've got to admit, this is even more satisfying than dunking Silverspinner in the waterfall."

Fernie said, "Yup," but really, she felt disappointed. Having always looked forward to being tall someday, she had been secretly kind of hoping that her own growth, which matched the growth of the carousel around her, would have given her more of a taste of what it would have been like to be a giant. But inside the control hub, there was really nothing to make her feel any different. As far as she was concerned,

Lemuel's shadow was the same size he had always been, and the control panel was the same size it had always been, and the battered toolbox was the same size it had always been, and she was the same size she had always been. Only the view out the sides of the carousel was any different, but not all that spectacular. It had largely been a glimpse up the sculpture's nostrils, which went away as soon as the carousel's edge bit into the giant October's skin, and then the view became a close-up of boulders flying upward.

Fernie took a little more satisfaction in knowing that Lord Obsidian's army of reinforcements, a massive solid wave of black that had been rising up the statue's body like an army of ants climbing an upright ear of corn, had stopped at the waist when they saw what was going on above them, and then retreated, terrified by a force that dwarfed even their evil master.

It would have been even nicer if she could have used the carousel's new size, and her own, to join the battle. But if she did, everybody still on the giant stone head would have seemed far smaller to her than the tiniest of tiny ants, and she probably wouldn't have been able to hop out and stomp on Lord Obsidian without also stomping on Pearlie, Dad, Not-Roger, Mr. Gloom, and Gustav with the very same step.

"The face is almost gone, Fernie. Want to saw off the arms next?"

"We don't have time," she said. "We have to get back and help our friends."

Lemuel's shadow saw the wisdom in this and hit the combination of buttons that should have returned the carousel to its intended size.

Instead, the lights went out . . .

"OCTOBERRRRRR!"

The cry came from behind Gustav, at the instant the giant head-quake ceased.

It was the cry of a man who had been pushed to his limits and was not willing to take any more—a cry so fearsome that Gustav knew at once why the human Howard Philip October had fled the owner of that voice for so long.

Flat on his belly because of the quake, Gustav peered over his shoulder and saw Hans Gloom standing alone, the anger he had carried with him for so long radiating from him like heat from a sun. He held a soldier's shattered sword in his right hand, and had curled his left into a fist so tight that the skin of his knuckles had turned white.

He looked different. Only a few minutes before, he had been forced to flee Lord Obsidian because that was his only choice against a figure that much more powerful than himself. But now he seemed bigger, more powerful, more of a threat. Maybe it was the shadow rising behind him, a hooded and faceless figure that looked like there was no place on any world that suited him more.

The sight was so formidable that the carousel animals retreated, and even Lord Obsidian's remaining minions, human and shadow, parted on either side, afraid to charge.

Lord Obsidian, who'd been about to make another grab for Mr. What, turned around and faced his old enemy, a foul delight on his crescent-shaped face.

Behind him, Mr. What staggered to his feet and ran to Pearlie, embracing her with the fervor of a man once again astonished that he was still alive to do it. Great-Aunt Mellifluous, who had managed to break free of her own opponent during the quake, took a step or two closer to them, but then stopped, clutching her hands together as she saw another phase of the battle about to begin.

All eyes fell on Gustav, the only person lying between two old enemies.

Lord Obsidian released a heavy sigh. "Very well. I suppose this is most appropriate. Get out of the way, boy. Give yourself a few extra minutes of life. Let me deal with this old business first."

Gustav rose to his feet and once again dusted himself off. "No."

"I don't hand out chances like they're candy, you foolish child. Take this one. I'll be happy enough to kill you once your father lies dead."

Again, Gustav said, "No."

Another sigh from Lord Obsidian, whose next look over Gustav's head, to meet Hans Gloom's eyes, was almost affectionate. "You should be proud, old friend."

"I wish I had the right to be," Hans Gloom replied, in tones just as deceptively friendly. "But thanks to you, I was never there to raise him. Whatever he's become, he's become without my help." He turned his attention to Gustav. "I love you, son. I may not know you yet, but I love you. I loved the idea of you before you were born and all those years I thought you were dead. I love you even more now that I see what a brave and true boy you are. And this is the only order I may ever have a chance to give you, as your father. Get out of the way and let us do this."

"No," Gustav said, more loudly, in the first act of disobedience he had ever shown his one living, flesh-and-blood parent. "I haven't come all this way to let you face him alone."

Hans's smile was broad and strong and full of joy. "I never said I'd be facing him alone."

As if in illustration, the hooded shadow behind him grew even larger, a storm cloud raging with what must have been years of pent-up fury.

Gustav still hesitated. Despite everything he had been through and everything he was capable of, he was still a boy, and boys don't always know the right thing to do. He didn't move at all until Penny Gloom's shadow, murmuring, "It'll be okay," broke from the ranks and took him by the arm to lead him out of the way of what had to happen.

Not far away, Not-Roger, who was reunited now with his own shadow, leaned in close to mutter something to Pearlie, who had just been once again reunited with hers.

"Wait. I've been keeping track. All the other shadows except Hans Gloom's are accounted for.

Caliban must be his missing shadow. Musn't he?"

Pearlie had guessed the same thing some time before, but now found herself unsure. "I don't know. I think so. Maybe."

"But I don't get it. So what if Hans Gloom has his shadow back after all this time? Having my shadow doesn't make *me* unstoppable. Having *yours* doesn't do you that favor, either. How could being reunited with *his* possibly make any difference?"

Pearlie What didn't understand it, either . . . but just when Gustav allowed himself to be led out of the way under protest, she suddenly *did*.

She grinned as she realized exactly what lay beneath Caliban's hood. "It wouldn't. That's not Mr. Gloom's shadow at all . . ."

Elsewhere, Fernie and Lemuel's shadow both found themselves trapped in a Cryptic Carousel that had lost all power and was now plummeting like any other object incapable of flight.

She screamed, "This isn't supposed to happen!"

"All those rock chips we just carved from October's statue! One of them must have gotten tangled up in the gears, or something!"

"What do you mean, 'or something'? Don't you know?"

"Not really! It could be anything! Maybe some mouse got in back at the house and chewed on the wires and we're only seeing the problem now! It's not like this thing has had a tune-up recently!"

"Can't you do something!?"

"I can do any number of things," Lemuel's shadow said. "I just don't know if any of them can stop us from crashing . . ."

Lord Obsidian strode toward his old enemy in no particular hurry, his long legs covering the distance in no time at all, his impossibly long arms drawing back for a blow that would drive most men to the ground.

For an instant, it looked like Hans Gloom and Caliban intended to stand there and let it come. But at the last instant they parted, Hans darting left and Caliban darting right. Hans swung his sword and sliced at Lord Obsidian's left knee. The blade only rebounded off Obsidian's substance, the impact not hurting him at all . . . but it didn't seem to be the attack Hans was counting on. *That* attack, taking place at the moment Obsidian was distracted, was Caliban's. The hooded shadow flung himself upward, grabbing Lord Obsidian by both wrists and shouting, "No more!"

Furious, finding Caliban a greater danger than the human being at his feet, Lord Obsidian ripped his arms free of Caliban's grip and flung the shadow aside. His swing was so powerful that Caliban should have sailed into the distance and plummeted into the Dark Country's mists, but instead the hooded shadow reversed direction in midair and flew back with the speed of a comet, this time racing toward Lord Obsidian's face.

"I told you!" Caliban yelled. "I have had more than enough of you! No more, I tell you! No more!"

Caliban became a sticky blob of ink adhering to Lord Obsidian's face. More specifically: He looked like a sticky blob of ink pulling in the material of Lord Obsidian's face. Shadow-stuff swirled between them, some being pulled toward Lord Obsidian and some being pulled toward Caliban—but for the first time, the shadow lord who had replenished himself with the material of other shadows was clearly facing another being capable of doing the same trick.

Lord Obsidian shrieked and tugged at the blob

and pulled out a long string of it and let go long enough for it to snap back and get a better grip on him. Whatever he did, Lord Obsidian could not get rid of it, and as his terrible fingers clutched at his face yet again, they succeeded only in finding and pulling back the material of Caliban's hood.

Everybody, friend and foe alike, gasped as they saw the face of the shadow screaming at Lord Obsidian that he had had enough.

As Penny had realized, it did not belong to Hans Gloom.

Instead, the features of the shadow who had called himself Caliban were that of a balding man with a large chin and forehead, whose visage had until recently towered over the Dark Country on the very statue where this battle was taking place.

It was the face of Howard Philip October.

Watching, gasping with all the others, Pearlie remembered the story Not-Roger had told them about Hans Gloom pursuing Hans Philip October through the wastelands of the Dark Country. October's shadow, horrified by what the human version was becoming, had fled, and never been seen again.

She had learned something from one of Gustav's acquaintances, the shadow of an unkind man named

Mr. Notes: that shadows were not necessarily like the people they resembled. Mr. Notes and his shadow hadn't been alike. The man had been petty and unkind, and the shadow well-meaning and decent, causing the shadow great mortification until the day he decided he wanted nothing more to do with the man and left him, forever.

Why had she ever assumed she would never see a case like that again?

<hr />

Elsewhere, Lemuel's shadow said, "Hold on. This is going to be close."

The enlarged Cryptic Carousel, which had been about to crush the castle on impact, leveled out and instead flew over it, skimming the plains of the Dark Country. On its way it passed over teeming armies comprising many, many thousands of shadows, stretching from horizon to horizon like a gray wave as they launched their counterattack on Obsidian's forces. They all cheered the carousel as it passed, a sound that was all by itself almost loud enough to drown out the other sound that had started to grow in the distance: the anguished scream of something not human.

Fernie had heard that sound before. "That's Lord Obsidian. We've hurt him again."

"You should be proud of that," Lemuel's shadow said. "When the history of the Dark Country is written, they'll sing songs of the day the statue lost its face and all good shadows knew the time had come to rise up and fight."

Fernie had trouble imagining such a song. *The shadow lost its face, la-la, it's time to win the race, la-la . . .*

She shook away the silly thought and said, "We have to shrink the carousel down to its proper size and get back to our friends."

"Yes," Lemuel's shadow said. "If I get the opportunity to check out the engines and clear out whatever small piece of statue grit is clogging the intakes, I'll be sure to do that. It probably won't take much more than a minute or two. But I think we'll be crashing first."

The carousel lurched, and slammed into something that made a horrid crunching noise before bouncing back into the air. Lemuel's shadow said, "Well, there goes a hill nobody's going to be using anytime soon. Hold on. This is going to be rough."

They slammed into the Dark Country's earth . . .

Many miles away, watching Hans Gloom battle Lord Obsidian with Caliban's aid, Not-Roger said, "I still don't understand this. Even if it is his own shadow, it's still only a shadow. What makes his shadow so unstoppable?"

Great-Aunt Mellifluous patted him on the wrist. "All by himself, his shadow isn't. His shadow was never able to stop him from committing his crimes; nor was his shadow ever strong enough to step forward and fight him, in all the years October has been Lord Obsidian. This required Hans Gloom's involvement, and with October's shadow in hiding and Hans Gloom on the run, we were never able to arrange getting the two of them in one place, until now."

"But I still don't understand—"

"Obsidian's not just being fought by one man and one shadow. He's being fought by a very special combination of beings: one man who was once his best friend and later his greatest enemy, and the shadow who embodies the better man he could have been. All at once, his best friend, his worst enemy, and the conscience he scorned. It's a deadly combination for a being whose greatest strength was always his belief in himself. Now shush your dear heart, and watch."

For Fernie, surviving the crash was a nice surprise.

Like a flat rock skimming the surface of a pond, the enlarged Cryptic Carousel had skimmed along the surface of the distant region known as the Rarely, scooping out a massive trench as it went, before finally coming to a stop at the base of the mountains that surrounded the land on all sides. (At this size, the carousel was actually as tall as some of those mountains.)

Fernie had survived the experience intact and had not been knocked unconscious, but for a few seconds she'd been a little too overwhelmed to do anything but lie where she was and recover as Lemuel's shadow entered the console and shouted up progress reports from the engine. To her ears, everything he said sounded like advisories that the freeblematzers were all gunked up with guacamole, or something.

She didn't feel better until the carousel shuddered, and from her perspective, the walls of the trench the carousel had carved seemed to shoot upward like the rapidly growing flowers shown in fast-motion in nature documentaries. By the time the carousel was back to its proper size, the walls of the trench were towering cliffs, and the trench itself was so wide that those cliffs were only distant gray lines on two sides.

The carousel had, she realized, just dug what the residents of the Dark Country would someday consider its Grand Canyon.

She grabbed one of the vacated poles and used it to pull herself to her feet. "Grandpa Lemuel!" she called. "How much longer?"

"Just a couple of minutes!" he said from down below, and rapid-fired another gibberish explanation about veeblefretzers and soufflés.

Concerned that this would be too long to make a difference, she stumbled forward and peered back along the track of the fresh canyon, willing her eyes to do the impossible and penetrate all the Dark Country's murk to whatever was happening on the statue's head.

Not far away, a patch of slightly blacker darkness scrambled down the cliffs and hit the base of the trench, screaming in rage as it charged.

It took her a second to recognize it, but when she did, her heart froze up as if grasped by an icy fist.

Oh no. Of all the stupid places to crash . . . !

"Grandpa Lemuel!" she shouted. "The Beast has found us!"

CHAPTER SIXTEEN
FERNIE VERSUS THE BEAST, AND GUSTAV VERSUS LORD OBSIDIAN

There was only one thing Fernie What could do, with Grandpa Lemuel's shadow still buried in the machinery doing what repairs he could: take the battle to the air.

She leaped onto the winged horse's back. "Up! Up, up! We have to lead it away!"

"I hear you," said the winged horse. "I was afraid we'd get through this whole battle without me ever getting to do anything."

The horse sprung from his assigned pole on the empty carousel into the air, swooping low over the dark landscape to charge the approaching Beast head-on. Just before its path crossed the monster's, it veered upward, coming so close to being seized by the Beast's terrible, shifting hands that Fernie felt the wind of the monster's fists grasping shut.

Below them, the Beast bellowed in rage, and

leaped. For Fernie, clutching the horse's mane for dear life, that leap looked like a roiling cloud of darkness, billowing upward like a thunderstorm somebody had seen fit to fire from a cannon. She caught a whiff of the thing's terrible breath, which smelled like what comes from the mouth of any dog that's eaten recently. She was certain that she and the horse were about to be snatched from the sky. But the horse's ability to fly was, in the end, just slightly better than the Beast's ability to leap, and the next thing she knew the Beast's great mouth receded again as the monster fell.

"That was close," the winged horse remarked.

"It has to be that close again," Fernie said. "If we can't keep that thing occupied, Lemuel's shadow won't have the time he needs to get the carousel running."

The winged horse shook its colorfully painted head. "Everybody's a critic," it remarked, as it dove again.

The bad news was that the Beast was faster than Fernie remembered it being from the couple of occasions in Gustav's house when she'd needed to run from it. Certainly, in the house she'd been able to stay just ahead of it with her own fastest run, but here in the Dark Country it was more than capable of keeping up with the full speed of a flying horse. Maybe it was angrier now. Or maybe whatever it used for food, whatever gave it strength and speed and unstoppable fury, was in greater supply in the Dark Country, and it really was more formidable now than it ever had been before. Whatever the explanation, it put on a burst of speed and managed to pull a metal feather or two from the horse's great flapping wings. It grabbed for Fernie, coming close to getting her until she ducked low in the saddle and let its great shapeless arm pass through the space where she had been. She was almost pulled out of the saddle by the breeze alone, but she held on, faced the prospects ahead, and saw a narrow canyon, one that promised only enough room for the horse itself. "There!" she cried. "Go there! There's not enough room for it to run alongside us in there!"

The flying horse warned her, "It'll just follow us! I'm not sure there's a way out once we're in!"

Fernie had to hug the saddle again to avoid another grab from one of the Beast's gigantic, shape-shifting arms. "I don't care!" she cried.

"I'm too busy to worry about it right now! Just go! *Our only chance is trying to lose it in there!*"

The winged horse obeyed . . .

On the ravaged statue's head, Lord Obsidian could not seem to remove the shadow who had called himself Caliban from his face, no matter how hard he thrashed. The shadow raged with a voice exhausted by the effort. "All those years I watched as you turned away every chance at happiness! All those years I suffered as I watched you betray all those who tried to be your friends! All those years I agonized as you became a monster! I could take no more!"

Lord Obsidian screamed the same way he had when the Beast had attacked him back in his throne room, a terrible yell that carried so far over the Dark Country that an answering cry came back in return, the cry of all those whom he had imprisoned and hurt and driven from their homes and worse, louder and angrier and ready to fight.

As Lord Obsidian stumbled around blindly, Hans Gloom evaded his stumbling and swung his borrowed sword at the backs of the villain's legs. This blow didn't do the villain any serious damage, but he seemed to feel it more than he'd felt any of the blows that came before it, because he roared and fell to his knees.

One of Lord Obsidian's guards suddenly realized his lord and master was actually losing. In a panic that might have been born of a last-minute attempt to impress the boss, he let out a cry and ran at Hans Gloom's back, readying his sword for a killing blow.

Gustav ran faster, scrambled up the man's back to his shoulder blades, and grabbed him by the ears, steering him away from the fight. The guard dropped the sword and fell flat on his belly only a few steps later.

"I surrender," the man said. "Force of habit."

Lord Obsidian, grasping for anything that would win him the battle, swung his arms again, his deadly fingertips passing within inches of Hans Gloom. Hans parried with a quick thrash of his sword, but stumbled back, crying out as his ankle twisted underneath him. Then Obsidian's fingertips found Gnulbotz. The guard screamed as his substance flowed into Obsidian's, giving the conqueror of the Dark Country the burst of strength he needed to seize the advantage in the fight.

Caliban, who had been growing larger and stronger and more powerful the more Lord Obsidian's substance drained into his, suddenly shrank to near-nothingness as Lord Obsidian claimed most of his substance for himself.

Lord Obsidian ripped Caliban away from his face.

All but emptied, Caliban fluttered to the ground, as weightless as an empty paper sack.

Lord Obsidian straightened. Everybody gaped at him, stunned by how suddenly he now seemed to be winning again. He reached out with one of his terrible arms and seized Scrofulous by the throat.

"No!" Scrofulous cried. "No, master! I've been loyal! Don't—"

Lord Obsidian shushed him. "Do not worry, my faithful servant. I'll make this painless."

Scrofulous faded into nothingness as his substance drained into Obsidian's body. None of the speeches he'd written, none of the words he'd spoken, had been enough to save him from being sacrificed the moment his master needed him. In seconds he was gone.

Obsidian plumped some more, like a dry sponge placed in water. There were still parts of him that looked weakened, almost emaciated, but he was still as big as a house, and still the most dangerous being in sight.

He stood all the way up, teetering on legs not quite strong enough to hold him.

"More!" he cried, gesturing at Krawg and Ravager. "Come to me. Give me everything you are so I can claim my victory!"

The two shadow guards, showing more intelligence than loyalty, fled, becoming just noisy gray blurs rocketing into the distance.

Nor were they alone. All around Lord Obsidian, shadow guards backed away, unwilling to flee, but also unwilling to be taken. Now that they'd seen their lord in a moment of weakness, whatever unshakeable loyalty they'd had was replaced by common sense—the practicality of vermin, waiting to see who came out on top.

Lord Obsidian swayed. "You will all be punished once this battle is done." His gaze fell on Gustav. "My greatest enemy was not enough to stop me. The conscience of my own traitorous shadow was not enough to stop me. Only the boy still stands, and he will not stand for long."

"You're one to talk," said Gustav. "I'll defeat you in less than one second."

Lord Obsidian took a single, staggering step toward him. "You're bluffing."

"If you say so," said Gustav. He picked up one of the battlefield's many abandoned swords. It was one of the largest swords lying around and was really too large for any boy to wield comfortably, even if that boy was as strong and as formidable as Gustav. Weight alone made it unsteady in his hands as he brandished it at the advancing Lord Obsidian, point foremost.

Were it only strength that determined the outcome of the battle about to conclude, Gustav would have been lost. But he had more than strength, and made that clear with what he shouted now: "Shadows! Those of you who fought with us and those of you who fought against us! Stay away from Howie! You don't want him to take you!"

All around, the shadows that had a choice retreated. Even those who had been working for Lord Obsidian before kept their distance, unwilling to give up what life shadows had in order to add to their master's fading glory. The shadows who had been Gustav's allies retreated with significantly greater reluctance, because they would have preferred to stay close and help him. But even they saw that as long as they stayed within Lord Obsidian's reach, they could be used to replenish his strength in his battle against Gustav, and so they retreated, too, all of them: Pearlie's shadow and Penny's, Mr. What's shadow and Not-Roger's shadow, and even Great-Aunt Mellifluous herself, all forming gray blurs as they fled to leave Gustav alone in a battlefield that offered no further food for Lord Obsidian's strength.

"You too," Gustav said. "All the humans."

Most of the human beings also retreated, those that were able. The ones in Obsidian's employ backed away, unwilling to get further involved in the battle between the tyrant and the boy, now that it looked like the tyrant could be beaten. The allies among them, Pearlie and Not-Roger and Mr. What, backed off a few steps as well, though not as many. They were unwilling to abandon their friend, and moved only because they sensed the importance of the moment. The carousel animals retreated with them, waiting.

Only Hans Gloom, immobilized by a twisted ankle and gazing at his son with the fearful eyes of a man who feared losing what he had just found, stayed where he was, his lips moving in fervent prayer.

Lord Obsidian stopped, swayed on his feet as if too weak to continue his advance, and then glanced away from the boy and toward the man.

"Uh-uh," Gustav warned. "He's hurt. I let him fight you first because he's been dealing with your nonsense longer than I have, and he had the right to go first if he wanted, but he's hurt now and can't fight you anymore. If you ever want to be seen as anything but a coward, you'll go for the one who can still fight. You'll go for me, and I'll defeat you in less than one second."

Lord Obsidian's gaze flickered back toward Gustav.

He marveled. "You really did come all the way to the Dark Country without a plan."

Gustav shrugged. "Plans are boring."

Lord Obsidian charged him.

Gustav thrust his stolen sword at what would have been Lord Obsidian's heart, had Lord Obsidian been human enough to still possess one.

It was a stronger and more assured attack than any that had been managed by Mr. What (who, for all his own courage, really hadn't known what he was doing) or Hans Gloom (who was many years out of practice). It pierced the gray darkness of Lord Obsidian's chest and likely would have killed a being of flesh and blood. But the weapon was just a sword, and the creature pierced by its point was not one that could have been slain by a sword. Lord Obsidian merely laughed and grabbed the blade between his long and serpentine fingers. The polished metal turned yellow and then rusted and then blackened and pitted, rotting into nothingness in no time at all.

All this happened in less than a second. Lord Obsidian had been toying with Mr. What, before. He had been enjoying Mr. What's helplessness. He was in no mood, right now, to take that much time with Gustav.

It was a good thing that by the end of that second, Gustav was no longer holding the sword.

Fully aware that the sword was useless, Gustav had let go of it the instant Lord Obsidian grabbed hold.

By the time the blade turned yellow, he was already darting between Lord Obsidian's planted feet.

By the time the blade rusted, he had already leaped, rolled, and grabbed the one thing lying on this battlefield that had proven capable of hurting Lord Obsidian at all.

By the time the blade blackened and pitted, he had already risen to his feet, holding Caliban, who was so drained by then he looked like nothing as much as a gray silk sheet drawn taut between Gustav's fists.

By the time the blade disintegrated into powder and dissolved in Lord Obsidian's hands, Gustav had returned at a dead run, raced up Lord Obsidian's back at a gallop, and slammed Caliban onto Lord Obsidian's pointed head, impaling him there.

By the time Lord Obsidian noticed that there was no boy at the other end of the sword he'd just destroyed, and realized that the weight on his head was Gustav on his hands and knees holding Caliban in place, Obsidian's strength was once again flowing back into Caliban's body.

By the time Lord Obsidian started to resist, Caliban was winning.

Lord Obsidian roared and reached for the top of his head, intent on freeing himself from the boy at least, but his terrible fingers passed through empty air. Gustav had moved faster than any not-half-shadow boy ever would have been able to, and ducked away from that awful grasping hand, popping his head back up as soon as he could be certain that the fingers had passed by without harm.

Lord Obsidian spun in place and reached for him again, but by now Caliban had grown so large on Obsidian's head that blindly reaching for Gustav was like groping for a bird perched on top of a giant wide-brimmed hat. At the same time, Obsidian had grown smaller. He screamed, aware that terrible defeat was coming for him.

Gustav saw that Caliban no longer needed his help holding on, and that staying in place any longer might even interfere with what needed to happen. He rose unsteadily, planted his feet against the spongy swirling mass of shadow beneath him, and leaped.

It was, of course, difficult even for a boy who could leap as far as Gustav to jump out of the reach of Obsidian's elongated arms. Lord Obsidian tried to pluck him from the air and came within inches of succeeding. But he was just a fraction slower than he had been only a few seconds ago, and Gustav flew beyond his reach.

Given the height of Obsidian's shoulders, Gustav should have suffered a bone-shattering impact with the ground . . . but Not-Roger caught him in cradling arms.

Gustav blinked up at his face. "Thank you."

Not-Roger looked dazed. "I think . . . I played football."

Gustav rolled out of his arms and landed on his feet, just as Lord Obsidian's screams became most despairing.

Caliban grew dark and full. Lord Obsidian withered further. He screamed and clutched at the black mass on his head, and shrieked and fell to his knees and tried to crawl forward to replenish himself with a shadow from the onlookers, but even the few allies that remained were backing away from him now, most of them wearing expressions of relief or disgust or disbelief that they'd ever bothered to follow a thing like him.

His terrible fingers clutched at Gustav, intent on aging him to dust.

Gustav backed away just a step, to avoid them, but by now it was easy. What had been Lord Obsidian could no longer move, and what had been Howard Philip October's shadow pinned him, growing thick as a tick on everything Lord Obsidian had been made of.

The battle was over.

The only question, for all who witnessed it, was this:

Was October's shadow, Caliban, any more trustworthy than the man?

CHAPTER SEVENTEEN
"WHAT'S A VALKYRIE?"

The creature who had started life as a man named Howard Philip October, and then gone on for several years as Lord Obsidian, now lay motionless, resembling a stick figure constructed from black pipe cleaners. He gave off a few wisps of sooty gray vapor, as some of what he was made of continued to bleed into the open air, but otherwise he lay unmoving, inert.

Unwilling to believe the nightmare was over, Pearlie said, "Is he dead?"

The now-towering shadow standing a safe distance from him, who they had all known as Caliban, shook his head. He bore all the features of the man October had been, and—now that he'd taken so much of Lord Obsidian's substance—was the same towering size, but where the face of the man had been marked with cold superiority and disdain for everything that lived, his was warm and filled with regret and sadness. He said, "You should know better than that by now. Shadows don't live and die the way people do. But drained the way he is, it will be some time before he regains enough substance to rise again."

"How long? An hour? A day?"

"Long enough," Caliban said, "that you should be able to find some safe place to dispose of him, if you don't waste too much time gathering all your friends and family together for your long journey home."

He looked like he wanted to say something else, but then his gaze faltered and he started to walk away.

Behind him, Gustav cried, "Wait a minute! That's it? You help us defeat the big bad guy and then you walk away? That's all?"

The melancholy shadow turned around and peered at Gustav with something very much like affection. "First, I have not defeated him. You all defeated him. You all stood up and refused to let him bully you into submission. I was just one of the tools you used.

"Second, I haven't finished him off. I never had that power. I have merely . . . stopped him for a while, so you can finish the job you began.

"Third, what else would you have me do? Change my appearance and pretend that I'm not who I am? Take Obsidian's place in the castle he built and rule in his stead? Go back to the world of light as your guest, and wander the halls of your house among shadows who remember the vile deeds of the man whose shape I still wear? Please, dear Gustav. Give me a suggestion I have not imagined. I am more than willing to entertain it."

Gustav's neighbors back on Sunnyside Terrace considered him to be the saddest little boy in all the world, but now he found himself facing what may have been the all-time saddest being: a creature of instinctive goodness who had no place in any world a shadow might walk.

But Pearlie had another question. "Where will you go, then? What will you do?"

October's shadow appeared not to have considered this at all, until the question was asked. Something impish tugged at the corners of his mouth. "Do you know the colorless lands surrounding the Dark Country?"

Pearlie had been to the place Gustav called the Dim Land, with some of the refugees fleeing Obsidian's wars. "Yes."

"I hear tell that awful nothingness extends far beyond any realms ever explored by either flesh or shadow, farther than anyone should ever go, or want to go. I believe I will start at the Dark Country's borders and start walking. I may walk for years, or even what your kind would consider lifetimes, through that empty place. But when I have either found a place that is better than 'nothing,' or traveled far enough to have left the evils committed here behind, I will stop."

"And then?" Pearlie insisted. "What will you do then?"

This appeared to have been the very first time the question had occurred to him, because he cocked his head and mused for a moment, and then allowed a little crinkle in his cheek to tug at the corner of his mouth.

"Why, then," he said, "I think I'll do what the flesh-and-blood October never could, and write some *happy* books."

He wasn't wearing a hat, but he gestured toward what would have been his hat brim as if to tip it in farewell, and spared a special nod for another shadow watching his departure in silence. "Farewell, Mellifluous."

"Take care of yourself," Great-Aunt Mellifluous
said. "And thank you."

October's shadow turned his back and began
to walk, fading with every step, until he was not
only transparent but almost invisible, and finally
until he was gone.

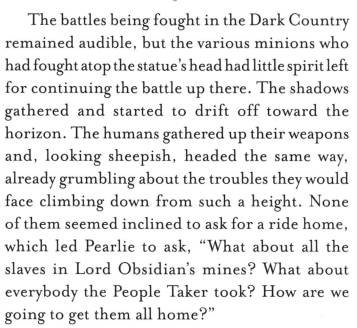

The battles being fought in the Dark Country
remained audible, but the various minions who
had fought atop the statue's head had little spirit left
for continuing the battle up there. The shadows
gathered and started to drift off toward the
horizon. The humans gathered up their weapons
and, looking sheepish, headed the same way,
already grumbling about the troubles they would
face climbing down from such a height. None
of them seemed inclined to ask for a ride home,
which led Pearlie to ask, "What about all the
slaves in Lord Obsidian's mines? What about
everybody the People Taker took? How are we
going to get them all home?"

Great-Aunt Mellifluous shook her head. "This
isn't like one of the stories in your books, child.
The defeat of the big evil villain doesn't make all
the world's problems go away in an instant. In

this case, the Dark Country is still in shambles, Obsidian's allies continue to fight for the cause he enlisted them for, and even if the battle below ends in immediate victory, the job of returning all those he imprisoned to their lives and reuniting them with their loved ones will no doubt go on for years to come. I suspect that there might be one or two smaller wars that follow in the aftermath of this one, just to get everything settled . . . and also that we may need many more journeys in the Cryptic Carousel before it's all done. But we have taken the first step. That is a great victory." She blinked, and focused on something in the distance. "Ah. Speak of the devil."

Two flying objects, one small and one large, had risen over the horizon that was at the front of the statue's head, and were coming this way.

One was the Cryptic Carousel, spinning merrily as it flew low over all those who had left the battle. It had sustained some damage in its vandalism of the statue's face and had lost most of the paint around its edges. Much of the Dark Country's shadow-stuff still clung to its surfaces, much but not all of it dissipating in little puffs of gray cloud as it flew closer.

The other object, a mere speck by comparison,

soon became recognizable as the carousel's flying horse, with Fernie in the saddle. As they watched, the horse skimmed the ground so Fernie could scoop up an object the departing soldiers had abandoned. When the horse rose back into the air, Fernie brandished the object she had found, point upward. It was a little sword.

While Fernie was still a fair distance away, Gustav grinned. "She's a Valkyrie."

Pearlie, who read a lot of books, too, but apparently hadn't read all of the same ones Gustav had, said, "What's a Valkyrie?"

Mr. What knelt to hug her, his eyes shining. "You are."

"Huh?"

"It means warrior woman, honey. And she is. Both my girls are."

A cheer rose from those who remained at the site of the battle as Fernie and the carousel drew close.

They landed, and what followed was an endless series of hugs in just about every possible combination: Fernie leaping down from the horse to rush forward and tearfully embrace her dad, then breaking away from him to embrace Pearlie, then the two of them hugging him again, and all three of them moving in a group to interrupt the private moment between Gustav, his father, and Penny's shadow so they could hug Gustav, too. Lemuel's shadow came out of the carousel and of course he had to be hugged as well, not just by Gustav and the girls but also by Hans Gloom, who almost broke down at the sight of his father's shadow and embraced him with the fervor of a man rescued from drowning.

This all went on even longer because the shadows also had to hug all the people and everybody had to hug Great-Aunt Mellifluous all together, just because. And then it went on even longer after that because Fernie suddenly spotted the lonely figure of Not-Roger, looking a little lost with no one but his shadow for company, because he'd spent so many years in the Dark Country and there was nobody around who had thought to be happy he'd survived.

There was no way that Fernie would ever allow that to go on, and so she whispered something to her sister and Gustav, and they ran to him together. The big man wept at the first affection he had received from any human being for longer than most of the people in this all-out hug-a-thon had even been alive.

The last combination left unresolved was the two fathers, and they faced each other from behind their respective kids, because they were two adults meeting each other for the very first time, and even in this kind of situation, grown-ups are never quite as comfortable with all that hugging as kids are.

One father stuck out a hand. "Hello. I'm Sidney What."

The other took it and said, "I'm Hans Gloom. I see our kids have already become friends."

"Yes," Mr. What said. "I think we're going to be great neighbors."

They nodded at each other, both wondering what else to say or do, and then by mutual agreement fell into what would not be the last hug between these people and shadows, during the journey to follow.

The only being who hesitated, as everybody else—shadows, mechanical animals, and human beings alike—boarded the Cryptic Carousel, was Not-Roger, who stood outside regarding it with both longing and fear.

The big man had never looked more like a child lost in a strange and unfamiliar place, unaware how to find his way home.

Gustav and the What girls hopped back off to speak to him, and Fernie said, "It's okay. We'll give you a ride back to the world of light, if you'd like."

He licked his lips nervously. "I'd . . . like that, Fernie. It's been so many years since I saw a sunrise, that I've forgotten what one looks like."

Still, he didn't move.

Gustav said, "What are you afraid of?"

"I . . . told you, back at the inn. I was never a very good man, in the world of light. I don't remember anything I did, but I think it's even possible that I might have been a bad person."

"There's an answer to that," Pearlie said. "Be a better one from now on."

He wiped his eye with the tip of his finger and went on. "But it's been . . . so long. I don't remember the number of the last year I saw, but I know it was before your grandparents were born, possibly before your great-great-grandparents were born. Everybody I ever knew is gone. The world I knew has moved on. I probably wouldn't even recognize it. What will I ever do? Where will I go?"

Gustav said, "If you don't come with us, you'll never figure it out."

Not-Roger considered that, then gave a nod that was more surrender than agreement, and followed them in uncertain silence.

Harrington the cat would not get the hug he deserved for a while, because he was a cat and he had just seen and heard more upsetting things than any cat ever likes to tolerate when there's serious napping to be done. When Fernie took his cat carrier from underneath the gorilla's hairy arm (thanking the gorilla for taking such good care of him) and opened the door, Harrington became a yowling black-and-white rocket, racing for a dark corner in the carousel's hub. Hugs, and petting, and sweet treats, and warm laps to lie in, were something he would doubtless have more than enough of in the future, but for right now he just wanted to be a cat by himself. This would pass.

Harrington the cat would not get the hug he

They took off, dangling Lord Obsidian's motionless form from one of the carousel's belly-mounted snares, as they flew low over the Dark Country's murk.

Most of the survivors of the battle on the statue's head sprawled exhausted in various places on the carousel floor, surrounded by robotic animals that had all returned to their places. Hans Gloom and the shadow of his murdered wife sat next to each other on the carousel's bench, speaking in low voices. Accompanied by his shadow, Not-Roger wandered from one immobile sculpted animal to another, running his paw-like fingers over their faces and marveling at bright colors he had almost forgotten. Great-Aunt Mellifluous stood at the carousel's edge, looking down through the clouds at whatever took place beyond, either smiling or frowning at whatever developments she found. Pearlie What, who had never been on the carousel before and had begged off the important strategy meeting in the hub in order to explore it, ran around in delighted girlish circles, spinning on the poles and acting far younger than her age, because she had just come from a place she had never expected to escape, and could not bite back the sheer joy of it.

In the carousel's hub, Gustav and Fernie held an important council with Lemuel's shadow, while the recovering Harrington did figure eights to claim permanent ownership of all their ankles.

Fernie said, "I'm still not happy about having to take Lord Obsidian with us."

Gustav replied, "You weren't around when October's shadow told us he would only be immobile this way for a while. What good will it do to leave him here, when he can just wake up and start where he left off? We *have* to take him with us and find some safe place to strand him where he can't ever get into any mischief again."

"Yeah," Fernie said, "but that's the problem, isn't it? He can wake up at any moment. Maybe years from now, but maybe only ten seconds from now. I don't want to be halfway home and suddenly have to deal with him wanting to come aboard so he can poke those awful fingers in our faces. I also don't want to take him anywhere too far out of our way. We have to hurry back for Mom. From what Obsidian said, she might be in real trouble."

Lemuel's shadow fluttered about the control console. "There's this, too. The Cryptic Carousel has many, many destinations programmed into its memory, but I'm afraid that many of them are inhabited by people—or other things that quite rightfully consider themselves people—who really don't deserve to have a menace like Lord Obsidian dropped into their backyards. I'm afraid my sense of responsibility won't allow me to just dump him in some random place and hope for the best, unless I can look around and know for sure that there's nobody close by he can try to conquer or kill, or any chance he can make his way to a civilization he can threaten. That would be unacceptable."

"So the only choice," Gustav said, not very happy about it, "is to take him to a place we've already been, a place far out of the way."

The place they all thought of at once had no name: a world of red skies, raging thunder, and four mountain spires emerging from a lower atmosphere of thick and impenetrable murk. In many ways it sounded too much like the Dark Country for comfort, and though the terrible spider-crone they'd fought there no longer resided at that address, Fernie had seen something far worse stirring below the clouds: an immense, evil, tentacled thing with a staring eye that she had hoped she would never see again.

But it wasn't like they had any other choice, not unless they wanted to spend half their lives looking for some place better. At least they knew how long it would take them to get there.

Gustav, Fernie, and Lemuel's shadow all spoke the name of the proper place at the same moment.

"Silverspinner's world!"

EPILOGUE
WHAT AWAITS IN GUSTAV'S FUTURE

The flight from the Dark Country to Silverspinner's world, through a shifting cloudscape of gray nothingness, was a lot like the flight in, except that there were more people to talk to and different things to be anxious about.

During the week or so the trip seemed to last, Gustav had many long and teary conversations with his father and with the shadow of the woman who would have been his mother, the three of them all catching up on the years they had missed. Fernie and Pearlie spent a lot of time hugging their father. Harrington calmed down and wandered from person to person, rubbing against ankles of both flesh and shadow, and thus, by cat logic, ensuring that everybody in sight belonged to him.

Beyond that, it was like any other long road trip through places where there really isn't all that much to see. If there hadn't been so much cause for worry about the forces Lord Obsidian had told them he had sent against Nora What on Sunnyside Terrace, they might have sung songs and played word games and fallen into lazy bored funks. Instead, they spent most of their time trying not to imagine the worst. Everybody also spent a great deal of time hoping that Lord Obsidian wouldn't wake up and cause some trouble before they got anywhere, but having that to talk about and nothing at all that could be done about it just made everybody grumpy.

Eventually, though, the Cryptic Carousel broke free into the sky over the world where Gustav and Fernie had fought the monstrous spider-crone named Silverspinner: a place with an endless sea of scarlet clouds that was only broken by four towering mountains.

Everybody aboard peered over the sides as Lemuel's shadow piloted the carousel toward a point between those four mountaintops, high above the tattered remains of Silverspinner's web. Only a couple of pink strands remained, the rest either dissolved by time or torn apart by the world's other creatures. The giant bird-creatures that had fled to the sky in fear of her now nested on those rocks by the thousands, making sounds that could have been caws and could have been the most terrible laughter any of the carousel's riders had ever heard.

Mr. What shuddered. "It's not much of an improvement over the Dark Country, is it?"

"No," Lemuel's shadow said. "It's not. The worst thing I can say about it is that he'll be right at home here. Anybody want to say anything else before we drop him off?"

Hans Gloom surprised them all by saying, "I would, if you don't mind."

They all waited as Hans stepped away from his place at the shadow-Penny's side, went up to the carousel's edge, and looked down. A wind had picked up, buffeting the lassoed Lord Obsidian, so they could all see the defeated tyrant's stick-figure form dangling above the mountain ledge they had chosen for his eternal prison.

"Once upon a time," Hans Gloom said, "I thought this man was a friend. My darling Penny thought he was a friend. Even after everything he's done, I've never stopped missing the man I once believed he was. I'll mourn that fictional man forever. But I hope I'll never again see the monster he turned out to be. That monster deserves to end his days in this terrible place." He turned to Lemuel's shadow. "That's it, I suppose."

Grandpa Lemuel's shadow pressed a button, and the lasso lowered the much-reduced Lord Obsidian to one of the nearest mountain's ledges. He showed no sign of recognizing that he had been released. The bird-things paid him no mind, either. The only sign that anything had taken notice of his arrival was a certain parting in the red clouds far below, which for an instant revealed coiled tentacles and a terrible slit eye, gazing up at them with emotions that nobody cared to read.

Hans Gloom found that he had one more thing to say. "That looks just like one of the creatures October wrote about in his books."

Gustav shuddered. "I know. I don't think he'll be too glad to meet it for the first time."

"No, son. I don't, either. But I think . . . maybe . . . he'll get some satisfaction out of having been right that there were such things in the universe. As long as he keeps his distance—and it doesn't get hungry."

Silverspinner's world was much closer to home than it was to the Dark Country, so the few minutes of flight that remained were filled with vocal worries about what perils might be awaiting them at home.

Then they heard the pop of displaced air and found themselves back in the Gloom house's carnival room, where the painted backdrops of sideshow amusements provided a stage setting for the carousel's assigned parking space inside the house.

None of them wasted any time gathering up their luggage, because none of them had brought any, unless Harrington's carrier counted. Instead they leaped off the ride and out the door and into one of the house's many corridors, where they could race toward the grand parlor and, they hoped, find some clue to the peril that faced Nora What.

They did not expect to find Nora What dressed in full safari gear, leading several shadows known to them, striding across the grand parlor in the opposite direction.

"Oh!" said Mrs. What.

"Mom?" said Fernie.

"Mom?" said Pearlie.

"Nora?" said Mr. What.

"Sidney?" said Mrs. What.

"Fernie!" cried Fernie's shadow.

"Girls!" cried Mrs. What.

"Gustav!" cried Gustav's shadow.

"Hives!" the kids yelled.

"Meow!" said Harrington.

"What great timing!" yelled Mr. Notes's shadow.

This was indeed great timing, and in the small explosion of excitement that followed, it became clear that Mrs. What, who was, after all, the official adventurer of the family, had proven as capable of dealing with the threat of the People Taker and the shadow army Lord Obsidian had sent to Earth to capture her as the rest of the What and Gloom families had been in dealing with equivalent menaces down in the Dark Country. By now, given how very often the various members of the What family had prevailed in their battles, with or without the help of Gustav Gloom or various assorted shadows, this honestly should not have been a surprise to anybody . . . and Mr. What actually felt the need to apologize at length to his wife for doubting her.

She sped through an explanation in one breath, saying that she had just experienced a harrowing adventure that had required her to run around the

Gloom house for what felt like days; that she and her new shadow friends had been chased by the People Taker and Ursula and their shadow army every waking instant; that they had come close to being captured a dozen times and closer to being killed even more; and that they had finally defeated their enemies and made it back to the grand parlor just in time to find the people she loved heading across the same room, toward her.

Though the precise details had to wait until all the hugging and kissing and weeping and, yes, meowing, were over and done with, and though there were also the many introductions to get out of the way, and they inevitably led to more hugging, Mrs. What ultimately offered her three-word summary of her adventure at the exact same time Gustav Gloom, her daughters, and even her husband used the same three words to summarize theirs.

"It was awesome."

Some of the details that came out, when everything calmed down a little, were not quite so happy. The People Taker had wound up falling back into the Pit to the Dark Country, and would likely stay there for a while, as there was no Lord Obsidian to send him back to the world of light for more mischief. Many of the shadow criminals had fled when it became clear that they were losing, though Ursula was one of those Mrs. What had succeeded in caging. The worst news, alas, was that the dire villain Hieronymus Spector had used the cover of the mass breakout to complete his own escape, and his current whereabouts and plans remained unknown.

This was, Great-Aunt Mellifluous declared, the most terrible of the loose ends, and it was one that would have to be dealt with someday.

Two weeks had passed after the family's return to the Fluorescent Salmon house on Sunnyside Terrace. Mr. and Mrs. What had straightened out the little bit of trouble caused by Fernie and Pearlie's missing the first few days of the school year, the girls had enjoyed their first week of classes and returned home eager for the weekend, and the What adults had fallen into the routine they always fell into between Nora What's expeditions: Mr. What writing a new book of the deadly hidden dangers of paper clips, Mrs. What laying out maps and travel guides as she tried to figure out what deadly risks her next TV special would require her to take.

It was the middle of a fine Saturday afternoon with nothing else happening, and the Whats were enjoying the peace and quiet of it all—a fine change from all the recent excitement—when they heard a knock on the door.

"I hope it's not Mrs. Everwiner," Mr. What said.

Their troublesome neighbor, driven by awful memories of her own misadventures inside the Gloom house, had started up a new campaign to tear it down and had knocked on their door four times already, trying to get signatures.

But when he opened the door, it was Great-Aunt Mellifluous.

"Hey!" Mr. What said, opening the door wide to let her in. "How are things in the Dark Country?"

He knew that Great-Aunt Mellifluous had been traveling back and forth to the Dark Country via the Pit, coordinating the relief efforts.

"Not as good as I would like them to be," she reported, as she drifted over the threshold, "but not as bad as I feared, either. The recovery will still take a while, but at least it's happening."

"What about Hans? Has he found his shadow?"

"Alas, no; there is no sign of the poor thing, so Hans will have to go on living without one for the time being. He says it'll be a while before he misses having one, as he's too occupied at home building a new family life with his son. I still have agents in the Dark Country, tracing the various rumors, and have no doubt that we'll be seeing a happy reunion before long. We haven't heard any more from the dastardly Hieronymus Spector, either. Wherever he is, whatever he's doing, he seems to prefer doing it in silence. We might be lucky enough to never hear from him again. But I doubt that. He is the kind of bad penny that always turns up.

"But I'm afraid this wasn't just a social call, dears. There's one last bit of business left over from all that unpleasantness in the Dark Country that I'll need to discuss with you. Nothing bad," she hastened to say, because Mr. What had gone pale. "Quite the opposite, in fact. But I hear from Gustav, who heard from the girls, that the two of you are still arguing over whether to sell your house and move your family away?"

"Well, not arguing," Mrs. What said, as she

took Mr. What's hand. "We've been disagreeing about it, a lot, but it hasn't become an *argument* yet."

"It's not something I'm happy about," Mr. What confessed. "I know what a great kid Gustav is and how much my girls love him, not to mention what a great example he is in all the ways that matter."

"They've been terrific for one another," Mrs. What agreed.

Mr. What said, "But I can't get past all the dangers my girls have been exposed to since we moved here. I don't want to turn around one day and find out that they've all disappeared into the Dark Country again, let alone to any of the places they can get to in that carousel thing."

"That's right," Mrs. What said. "And I keep saying that the kids have shown us what an unbeatable team they make, and what a shame it would be if we failed to respect that, or broke up their friendships."

Great-Aunt Mellifluous nodded in deep understanding. "You're both right, and I have no intention of arguing with either one of you. But if moving away is actually still under discussion, perhaps I can help you make a decision. If you're up to coming across the street for a short visit, may I show you something that neither of you knows about yet that should make a special difference?"

Mrs. What agreed at once. Mr. What, who remembered all the trouble he'd had the last time he'd popped over to the Gloom house for just a few minutes that somebody promised him would be perfectly safe, needed a little more persuading, but eventually, he gritted his teeth and agreed to go, holding his wife's hand for extra safety.

They crossed the street, passed the Gloom estate's gate, and went into the yard, where they collected Gustav and their girls (who were having the latest in a long series of picnics). On the way up the walk they said hello to Not-Roger, who had taken on the name Roger Knott and was settling in just fine in his new position as the Gloom family groundskeeper.

Dealing with Hives at the door, and allowing him to aggravate them a little just so he could have some satisfaction in his work, they proceeded together down the long entrance hall. They collected another old friend when they ran into Mr. Notes's shadow, who for some reason seemed to be having trouble suppressing one of the most conspiratorial smiles that any of the Whats had ever seen.

Ascending one of the grand parlor's many stairways, to a balcony that Fernie said she'd walked before, they followed Great-Aunt Mellifluous through a doorway Fernie said she'd seen before, into a room that Fernie said she'd visited before.

There they found Hans Gloom and Penny's shadow, waiting with grins almost as poorly concealed as the one Mr. Notes's shadow also struggled to hide behind his hand.

As Mr. and Mrs. What stood blinking at the array of paintings that hung as far as their eyes could see, Great-Aunt Mellifluous said, "I have told Gustav many times that there are no prophecies. The future is never written. Destiny promised us no chosen heroes to rid all creation of Lord Obsidian. When the time came for that to happen, it fell to a small group of friends and family, all doing the absolute best they could for the ones they loved, with no guarantee of victory.

"Always, everywhere, history doesn't happen until it happens.

"But that doesn't mean it's never possible to see what the future might be, or even what it will probably be.

"That's the force at play in this room, my friends. This is the Gallery of Possible Futures, where the shadows of what *might* be, what *should* be, and what should *never* be allowed to be are all captured on canvas, for the eyes of any who come here.

"Fernie, I know that you have been in this room before, and had its nature explained to you. On that occasion, I understand you saw a painting of the terrible place the world of light would become if Lord Obsidian were ever permitted to succeed in his mad ambitions. Is that true?"

Fernie gulped. "Yes."

"I have spent much of the last two weeks searching for that painting, and have so far not succeeded in finding it. If the future it foretells is still even remotely possible, it may still hang in some out-of-the-way alcove, but somehow I believe that the chances of any of us ever seeing it again are now too remote to worry about. We need not speak of it again.

"Still, there is another painting we should revisit, one I know that you have also seen before, and one very well known to the shadows with us who watched Gustav grow up." Great-Aunt

Mellifluous turned to Penny's shadow. "You know the painting, don't you, dear?"

For some reason, Penny's shadow could not stop grinning. "Yes. It's always been one of my favorites."

Great-Aunt Mellifluous escorted the two families to another painting Fernie found familiar, having stopped before it during the adventure of the Four Terrors.

This painting seemed to depict Hans Gloom and a beautiful redheaded woman in mountain-climbing gear, atop a pillar of rock with a vast brown desert far below. The sky behind them was a brilliant cloudless blue, and the sun looked warm on both of their bright shining faces. It looked like the most beautiful of beautiful days.

Great-Aunt Mellifluous asked, "Fernie? Do you understand what this painting shows?"

"Sure," said Fernie. "That's Mr. Gloom, and some woman I've never seen before."

"You're wrong about that being *that* Mr. Gloom," Great-Aunt Mellifluous said. "You are right about that being a woman you've never seen before, not yet at least, but that's not Hans. That's Gustav."

Fernie gave the grinning man in the picture

another look, and could not make a face that cheerful look like an older version of the Gustav she knew, no matter how hard she tried. "Are you sure that's not his dad? It looks just like him."

"It does look almost exactly like Hans, and if this painting hung anywhere else in the house, I would indeed be tempted to believe it was him. But you forget that this is a gallery of the future, dear, and the man in the picture is several years younger than Hans is now. He has fewer lines on his face and more color in his hair. Whatever the future has in store for Hans, and I hope that it will bring nothing but happiness, I suspect that he will not be fortunate enough to age backward. No, I have studied this painting for many years, down to every pore on this man's cheeks. I'm certain. That's Gustav."

"But that can't be Gustav," Fernie insisted.

"Oh, no?" Great-Aunt Mellifluous asked. "Why not?"

"Because we all know that Gustav would die if he ever left this estate. He would *evaporate*. The man in the painting is out in the sun climbing a mountain. He even has a *tan*. He *can't* be Gustav."

"And yet he is," Great-Aunt Mellifluous said. "In this painting's possible future, Gustav is out in the world, walking in the bright sun without fear. Somehow, something happens to him between now and then, something that none of us can even guess at, that makes such a blessing possible. Maybe it's another adventure. And maybe it's just time."

Fernie glanced at Gustav, who was so stunned by this development that he'd taken a step back, and been caught by his flesh-and-blood father and his shadow mother. "Out in the *sun*," he whispered. "With *people*. Seeing something of the world other than *this house . . .*"

It seemed to be too much for him to take in all at once, but Fernie had never been happier for another person in all her life. She was overjoyed to be with him when he got this news, and could only hope with all her heart that this particular possible future came true. "Okay," she said, conceding the point. "I hope you're right. But then, who's that woman with him?"

"Ah," said Great-Aunt Mellifluous, and now there was something special about her smile, something that spoke of life's unexpected gifts. "You will notice that both the man and the woman in the painting wear wedding rings. From that evidence, I venture that she's Gustav's possible future wife . . . and, judging from many of the other paintings you'll find around here if you look hard enough, not just a world-famous adventurer alongside her husband, but also the possible future mother of his children."

What followed was an extremely long moment of silence as the various gathered friends and family absorbed this information and tried to put together what Great-Aunt Mellifluous was implying.

Of them all, Pearlie was the very first to get it, with a delighted yelp of, *"No way."*

Great-Aunt Mellifluous smiled at her. "I believe this is where you children would say, 'Yes, way.'"

"What?" Fernie demanded. *"What!?"*

Gustav didn't get it, either. "Yes! *What?"*

Pearlie was positively bouncing. "Come on! How can the two of you not see it?"

"SEE WHAT?" Gustav and Fernie cried together.

Everybody in the room seemed to get it now, except for those two; they simply didn't have a clue, and didn't seem capable of getting a clue, no matter how obvious the import of the painting had just become to everybody else.

Not far away, backing up against the nearest

wall, a stunned Mr. What murmured, "Nora?"

She didn't look one bit less dazed than he did. "Yes, dear?"

"You win. We're not selling our house. Not now, or ever."

Their hands met, and her fingers twined with his.

She said, "I know. But maybe we can have a little talk about painting it."

(This is the famous poem that Gustav understood a little better than Howard Philip October did, provided in case any reader is curious.)

OZYMANDIAS
By Percy Bysshe Shelley

I met a traveller from an antique land
Who said: Two vast and trunkless legs of stone
Stand in the desert. . . . Near them, on the sand,
Half sunk, a shattered visage lies, whose frown,
And wrinkled lip, and sneer of cold command,
Tell that its sculptor well those passions read
Which yet survive, stamped on these lifeless things,
The hand that mocked them and the heart that fed:
And on the pedestal these words appear:
"My name is Ozymandias, king of kings:
Look on my works, ye Mighty, and despair!"
Nothing beside remains. Round the decay
Of that colossal wreck, boundless and bare
The lone and level sands stretch far away.

ACKNOWLEDGMENTS

You would not now be seeing this book without the persistence of agents extraordinaire Joshua Bilmes and Eddie Schneider of the Jabberwocky Literary Agency. You would not now be enjoying the same experience free of verbal land mines and other clutter without the ace red pens of copy editor Kate Hurley and editor Jordan Hamessley. You would not now be oohing and aahing over the illustrations without the genius of artist Kristen Margiotta. You would not now be holding the divine artifact in your hands without designer Christina Quintero. You might have no idea the book exists without the fine work of publicist Tara Shanahan. You would not now be seeing any books from me at all without the patience, love, and constant encouragement of my beautiful wife, Judi B. Castro. You would not now be seeing a human being with my name and my face were it not for my parents, Saby and Joy Castro.

Most of all, thank you to all the young readers who have expressed their appreciation for Gustav and Fernie and their world.

ADAM-TROY CASTRO has said in interviews that he likes to jump genres and styles and has therefore refused to ever stay in place long enough to permit the unwanted existence of a creature that could be called a "typical" Adam-Troy Castro story. As a result, his short works range from the wild farce of his Vossoff and Nimmitz tales to the grim Nebula nominee "Of a Sweet Slow Dance in the Wake of Temporary Dogs." His twenty prior books include a nonfiction analysis of the Harry Potter phenomenon, four Spider-Man adventures, and three novels about his interstellar murder investigator, Andrea Cort (including a winner of the Philip K. Dick Award, *Emissaries from the Dead*). Adam's other award nominations include eight Nebulas, two Hugos, and three Stokers. Adam lives in Miami with his wife, Judi, and three insane cats named Uma Furman, Meow Farrow, and Harley Quinn.

KRISTEN MARGIOTTA has been creating spooky, creepy images since her early childhood. Now as an adult, she explores similar themes with more depth and further enjoyment. Since 2005, Kristen has been working as a freelance illustrator, painter, and art instructor. She finds that her roles as visual artist, illustrator, and instructor influence and strengthen each other, and she enjoys the challenges and rewards that come from these endeavors. Kristen is the illustrator of *Better Haunted Homes and Gardens*, and her work can be found in the homes of collectors throughout the country. She continues to exhibit in galleries, museums, and local events. Kristen resides in Delaware with her husband, Lee, where they both are actively involved in the art and music communities. Learn more at www.kristenmargiotta.com.